The Curiosity of Innocence

By

Tony Surgey

This book is dedicated to anybody whose past still haunts them and dictates their future. Whether that be in their childhood or early life.

It is so important for your life to have strong foundations, in order for you to move forward. People who have never faced these issues will try and empathise but will never fully understand your pain.

May you find the strength to fulfil your hopes and aspirations? We have no control over the past and very little over the future. Just try and enjoy the here and now and be all you can be.
Peace, happiness and love to you all.

Tony Surgey

Chapter 1
In the shadows of God

John looks up at his mother and smiles. "This cakes lovely mum, can I have another piece?
"You can darling, but save some for when your dad comes home." John looks over at the window wishing his dad would come home. It's late October and the wind is driving rain against the window so hard it was making the single paned glass flex. Staring at the window and wishing his dad would come home, was something, John was used to. It wasn't like his dad was working away or a knowingly unconcerned absent father. Quite the opposite. John's dad was a clergyman and it was his devotion to the church and the people of Forchester, that was keeping him way. The 10 year old John just wanted the attentions of his father, more than anything in life.

Two hours later, his dad finally arrives home. He is a man in his early 40s by age, but in his early 60s by manner. He is short and chubby, with a protruding nose and thinning hair. This was 1984 not 1964. While other fathers were watching Miami Vice and entertaining their off springs propensity for Spandau Ballet, Wham and Duran Duran. The Reverend James Bryant strictly pipe, slippers and some boring documentary.

Kate passes a plate of beef stew and dumplings to her husband. While her husband grabs the remote control from the arm of the sofa. He points it at the TV and presses a button in vain. He bangs the remote against the outside of his thigh and leans forward. The very presence of a TV remote in 1984 saved the user perhaps three to four steps to manually turn the TV over.

"John, it's 8.30 you need to get to bed. You have got school in the morning."

John can hardly believe his father, wanted him to go to bed. He hadn't uttered a single word to him since he returned home. John walks over to give his dad a hug and James pushes him to one side, his presence blocks his view of the TV.

"Goodnight dad."

"Oh, Goodnight god bless. Don't forget to say your prayers."

"I will dad."

John, takes himself off to bed. He wants to be a happy child, but feels lonely and unloved.

"You could have let John stay up a little longer. He just needs his dad sometimes."

"I am tired Andrea and I want some time to myself. It's been a hard day. I have had three funerals today followed by visits to parishioners in need of prayer."

"Your son is in need too, James."

"I do my best, my father was out all the time and I wasn't needy like John."

James turns the TV up in defiance to watch his documentary.

Morning arrives and John is dressed in his school uniform and is sat at the dining table, eating Weetabix. James ruffles his fine blonde hair, on the way out of the door.

"Have a good day at school son."

"You too daddy."

This small act of affection and some acknowledgment warmed John's heart He allowed himself a smile. The walk to school was a short one and John soon found himself outside the gates of St Thomas primary school. The village school was 100 years old, made of stone, with arched windows. In keeping with the nearby St Saviours church. If only John knew what irony was, he would have found it ironic that he spent his school day so close to his dad. The day passed quickly and without incident. John walked home with a class mate called David.

"Is it true that your dads a vicar."

"Yes, he works over there."

John points in the direction of St Saviours.

"Do you have to go to church and do a lot of praying then?"

"Sometimes."

"My dad doesn't believe in God. He says it just a load of rubbish from thousands of years ago."

"It's wrong, not to believe in god. How are you supposed to go to heaven?"

"It's easy, he doesn't believe in heaven either. "

To John's relief, he was now outside his front door and all the silly no God nonsense

can stop now.

"See you tomorrow David."

"You too, God boy."

This upset John a little, because he is quite a sensitive boy. John opens the front door to The Vicarage and walks in.

"Hello mum."

"Have you had a good day at school darling?"

"Yes mum, we made some scary ghosts out of clay for Halloween."

"That sounds nice, I hope they aren't too scary."

"I think we can bring them home next week, when they have been in the kiln and painted."

John was still thinking about what David had said to him.

"Mum, I walked home with a boy from my class, when he found out what daddy does for work, he started calling me God boy."

"Just ignore him darling, people always mock things they don't understand."

John goes up to his room and starts looking through his junior bible. He knows this will please his dad. He starts to read the story of the prodigal son, which puts him in mind of David. James is unexpectedly home early. John can hear his footsteps coming up the stairs. The bedroom door opens and James walks in.

"Hi son, how was your day?" "Fine thanks dad, I enjoyed school and got 10 out of 10 in my times tables test."

"That's brilliant. What are you reading?"

"The story of the prodigal son dad."

"A good story John, but it is still better not to be like the prodigal son."

"What do you mean dad?"

"God would rather you choose the right path than forgive you for taking the wrong path."

"Dad I am scared, that one day I might do things wrong and God will not forgive me."

"If you don't, there will never be anything for God to forgive."

James gives John a stern look and walks off. John feels like he can never do enough to please his dad. He had just been corrected for something he had not yet done. He throws the bible across the room in a momentary fit of rage. The dust cover on the bible tears slightly in the corner and John feels bad. He knows his dad would not be pleased if he knew.

The last year at Forchester junior school flew by and John was preparing for life in high school. He would have to travel the 5 miles to school on the bus. The particular high school in question was Perthwaite Senior School for boys. James did not want his son being distracted by the presence of girls during his teenage years. John's mother had pleaded with her husband to let John go to the same high school as his friends. James always wanted the best for his son, but didn't always appreciate the ramifications of his decisions.

It's late August 1985 and John is trying on his school uniform, much like many kids across the length and breadth of Briton. He looks smart in the bright yellow blazer trimmed with blue. If it wasn't bad enough having to attend a school not of his choice. He now has to get on the bus looking like a Pina Colada.

"You look lovely John."

"Thanks mum." John tries to look proud but inside he is really crying.

"Nice to see you wearing a tie. I so disliked those polo shirts, you wore in your last school."

The green and purple striped tie, was no better than the ghastly blazer. The whole ensemble was finished off with a purple cap. In the big scheme of 1980's clothing this was an incredibly awful outfit. John would have drawn less attention to himself, if he had dressed in Boy George's full Karma Chameleon regalia.

"I went to Perthwaite John, but I never looked that smart."

For a moment, John looks proud. Then he catches a glimpse of himself in the mirror and realises once again how ridiculous he looks. Oh well, it's only 5 years. This equated to half his life and would feel like forever. The next few weeks flew by and it was soon time for Perthwaite, day one.

The bus from Forchester to Perthwaite was a decrepit old Leyland single decker in mid green with blue striped seats. By the time John had made his way onto the bus, there were no more than a handful of pupils on-board. John took a seat and stared out of the window at his former school mates making their way to the preferred high school for the area. He felt sad and would have given anything to be amongst his peers.

The journey to Perthwaite seemed to last forever, but in reality, was only around 30 minutes.

All sorts of thoughts were going around in John's head like a pin ball machine firing off in all directions. What will it be like? Will he make friends? Are the teachers strict? Can he please his dad by fulfilling his potential? To the outside world John would have appeared to be in a daze.

Perthwaite was a Victorian building with big imposing wrought iron gates and a sign in the same canary yellow as the blazers. John took a big gulp as the bus pulled up and he stood in line down the aisle waiting to get off. The driver opens the door.

"Good luck boys, enjoy your first day."

John thanks the bus driver for his kind words and makes his way off the bus. Perthwaite is not a public school but is strongly affiliated and partly funded by the Church of England. The teachers meet the new starters at the gate.

"Armstrong-Jones, Jackson, Bryant, please follow me."

All three boys mutter a token "Sir" and follow on behind.

Perthwaite is an historical building nearly 300 years old with some grand architecture. The walls are covered in pictures of former classes and sports teams. Everything seems traditional and like nothing has changed in the 300 years since it was built. In modern terms like a council house Hogwarts minus the magic.

As John walks around, he feels nervous and overwhelmed by the pressures of having to live up to the schools exacting standards.

The boys are directed into a classroom and meet their new form teacher. The teacher in question is Mr May.

"Good morning boys, my name is Mr May I am your new form teacher. I am fair but firm, all I ask is you try hard and treat the staff and each other with respect."

Mr May was the typical teacher off the day. He was in his early 50s and had been at the school some 25 years. He had little interest in promotion and was happy to churn out a never-ending line of potential high achievers. His once jet-black hair was now greying and he peered over his silver rimmed glasses. His brown corduroy jacket complete, with leather patches on the sleeves had seen better days.

The class of around 15 boys are sat behind the typical 1960's front opening wooden desks that were in use all the way through the 80's. One of the boys at the rear of the class was day dreaming and staring out of the window. Mr May walks over and opens the desk, before banging it back shut, causing all the boys to jump.

"What have I just said, lad?"

The boy just looks up at Mr Bryant with a tearful look in his eyes.

"You don't know do you! I said respect the staff and each other."

The boy relies "Yes sir!" through his quivering lips.

"Now everyone is back in the room and not obsessed by the fascinating school field, I will carry on. In a while we will be going around the school so you will have an idea where everything is. Later this morning I will give you your timetable and you can introduce your selves to each other.

"Sir!"

"Yes, Bryant."

John was used to being referred to by his first name not his last and it all felt so very formal.

"What do you mean by introduce ourselves?"

"I don't know you and to the best of my knowledge you don't know each other. So all I want you to do is tell the class something about yourself. Something like, my name is John and I went to so and so school before here. I like listening to chart music and playing football. "

"Thank you sir."

"Thanks for asking! It is very important to ask questions if you are unsure."

The boys completed their tour of the school. How much they had managed to take in was questionable.

"Right boys tell me about yourselves. "Jackson! You got first."

"My name is Robert Jackson and prior to coming to Perthwaite I was at Rockley Junior School. I like to play cricket in the summer and make model aircraft."

"Thank you Robert."

The class introduce themselves in turn, until its John's turn.

"My name is John and I went to Forchester School before coming to Perthwaite. I enjoy reading my bible and saying prayers with my dad."

"Is your dad particularly religious John?"

"He is sir, because he is a Reverend at St Saviours Church in Forchester. "

"That's wonderful John. Thank you class that was very helpful and I feel like I know you all just a little more."

John was surprised, that the day passed without reference to his prayer saying or his father's occupation. The bus journey back home felt a little more pleasant than the journey to school. The best part of getting home from school was removing the canary blazer and purple cap.

John soon came to terms with the bus journey and the demands placed on him by Perthwaite life. He had also formed friendships with some of his class mates. The first day anxieties were replaced by familiarity and a sense of belonging. The only constant pain in John's side was his blessed blazer.

At home John's parents James and Kate, were going through difficult times. James devotion to St Saviours and the Church of England was getting in the way of their marriage. They were struggling to keep their difficulties under wraps and away from John. In the presence of John the problems would mainly manifest themselves in the form of long periods of silence between the couple. John for the best part was pretty oblivious to it all.

It's the weekend and John had been out playing football with friends. He returns home, his parents are both in the garden. Kate is trying to cut back a rose bush, but is struggling to reach the top.

"James can you go into the shed and pass me the steps please?"

John is sat on the patio making changes to his Sunday sermon. He completely blanks his wife and Kate is now on her tip toes trying to cut the hedge. John walks through the back gate which slams shut behind him causing Kate to jump. She loses her footing and falls into the rose bush. She winces as the thorns scratch and pierce her skin. James is still engrossed in his work and doesn't even raise his head. John rushes over to his mum.

"Are you ok mum? You are bleeding."

Kate has a number of scratches to her hands and arms. Her cornflower yellow dress was ripped near the sleeve. But James still failed to acknowledge her presence, let alone her misery.

"Dad mums hurt!" James finally looks up and walks over.

"What did you do?"

"I fell into the bush, because I was trying to reach the top."

"Why didn't you get the steps?"

"I asked you to get them but, you just ignored me.

Chapter 2
Goodbye Mum

John feels anger towards his dad. What is so important that can't wait for a few moments? Kate starts to cry which is a result of her injuries, her damaged dress and her husband's ambivalence towards her. This just arguments Johns anger towards his father. John gives his mother a reassuring hug, before helping her walk back in to the house. By now James has returned to his sermon. This was the first time John had realised how cruel his god loving, righteous father could be.

The next 5 years at Perthwaite were a breeze for John compared to dealing with the ever growing tensions between his parents.

John is in his GCSE, Religious Education exam, which was compulsory at Perthwaite. He was an exemplary student in all subjects. However RE was his forte, because of his father's pre-occupation with all things religious. John was making his way through the 90 minute exam with consummate ease and was more than 80% finished with lots of time to spare. John feels a tap on his shoulder. He turns to see an invigilator telling him to make his way out of the hall. As he leaves the hall he is greeted by the school principle who is in the company of a police officer.

"John can you please come into my office."

John is rightly confused and upset at having to leave his exam. He makes his way into the office and is offered a seat by Mr Wilson, the Principle.

"Hello John, I am PC Rogers from the Rochester Neighbourhood Policing Team."

John takes a gulp. "Hello pleased to meet you."

"I am sorry to tell you this John, but your mum was found dead this morning."

John's whole world has collapsed with the delivery of one sentence, tears fill his eyes and his pulse begins to raise.

"What happened?"

"Apparently the postman could see water running from under the door of your house. He alerted a neighbour, who is a friend of your mums. She knocked, but could get no answer. They entered your house and could see water cascading down the stairs. They then made their way to the bathroom, where they found your mum dead in the bath with the taps running and her wrists cut."

John begins to cry uncontrollably. What could be so bad that she would kill herself?

"John we found this. It's a letter from your mum addressed to you. It was on the sink in the bathroom."

The police officer hands over the letter to John. He pauses for a minute, curious but frightened. Eventually he rips open the envelope and begins to read.

"John, by the time you read this I will be dead. I am so, so sorry son, I love you more than words can ever say and I cannot begin to tell you how proud I am of you. I suppose I owe you an explanation, has to why I won't see you grow up, get married and have children."

"John's tears begin to fall ever more intensely as he reads this line.

"I do not love your father. He has made my life a living hell over the past 10 years. If he cared for us the way he does about the church I would still be alive today. You don't know this, but I have asked him for a divorce so many times over the last six months. He just says no and quotes the marriage vows. TILL DEATH DO US PART.? Well he has made it happen now. Please remember I will always be in your heart and your head as you will be in mine. I am sorry for doing it on the day of your RE exam, but if it pisses your father off then I am happy."

John drops the letter to the floor and leans forward with his head in his hands.

"I think that's it for today for you John. Because of the exceptional circumstances I will contact the exams board and see if I get you a resit."

"Don't worry sir. I don't want to do any exam that involves the very thing that contributed to my mum's death."

Mr Wilson puts a reassuring hand on Johns shoulder.

"I understand."

Over the next few months John had little time for his father and the childhood bible had been burnt to a cinder shortly after the death of his mother. John was now approaching his seventeenth birthday and he was starting to show intolerance and defiance towards James.

"Are you coming to the charity function tonight to help out?"

"No sorry dad, I am going out to a house party with some friends."

"I hope there will be parents there and no alcohol John."

"It's Mark Ibbotson's house, his mum and dad will be there."

This was a semi truth. Mr and Mrs Ibbotson were going out for a meal and would be away from the house for a number of hours. They were happy in the fact Mark was responsible and only a few months from his eighteenth birthday. They would be home fairly early and had restricted Mark to only inviting a handful of guests.

"Ok John I will drop you off."

"Thanks dad."

John is dropped off at Mark's house, luckily for him the Ibbotson's car is still outside giving the impression they are still in even though they have been picked up by a taxi.

John was still painfully shy and lacked confidence. He is a typical teen, skinny and struggling to keep the acne at bay. Gone was the short back and sides, insisted on so long by his dad. The hair was now longer and showed mullet potential. His top lip had the faint hint of facial hair. John knocks on the front door and is greeted with.

"Just come in mate."

Mark was in the kitchen with the boy who had many years ago given him such a hard time about his dad being a member of the God squad. John already socially unskilled now felt very uncomfortable.

Chapter 3
My broken heart

"Oh, hi Mark! This is Dave."

"I think we have already met."

"I remember you from Forchester School."

"Just waiting for a few more to come. I have got some cider and dad won't miss a few cans."

Mark walks over to the Technics stereo in the living room and puts on a mix of 80s music. The distinctive air raid siren beginning from Frankie's, two tribes fills the three-bedroom semi. John takes a small swig of cider, knocking his head right back but only partially swallowing to make out he is drinking more than he is. Even at nearly 17 his dad would not take kindly to him going home blind drunk.

The change of music to Madonna's, Material girl, coincides with the arrival of two more guests. Emily Watts and Georgia McCarthy enter the room. They were both in the year above John at Forchester. John had not seen them for 5 years and they had both changed. Gone was the pigtails and gingham blue dresses in favour of outrageously wild permed hair and the fluorescent madness of 80s party clothing. Georgia had a reputation for being one for the boys. She loved male attention and she got it with her shorter than short skirts, low cut tops and a manner that can only be described as slutty. Her shapely body, over done makeup and over the top hair further cemented the slutty girl image in people's minds. She was just what a teenage boy dreamt of 99 percent of the time.

Within seconds of entering the room she grabbed Mark and they started to dance.

Emily knows that Georgia has a crush on Mark and takes the time to pick up the stylus from the stereo and place it on the beginning of something slower and smooches. The unforgettable saxophone solo rings out, and proceeds the melodious voice "Time can never mend the careless whispers of a good friend." Georgia pulls Mark closer and jokingly grabs his bum with both hands. Mark is still sober and more interested in his friends and being a good host than cracking onto her. Georgia soon turns her attentions to the cider, pouring herself a pint glass full.

"So Mark if you are going to be frigid all night, who else is coming to dance with?"

"Well Simon and Andy Johns were supposed to be coming, but so far it's a no show."

"I will just have to get you pissed then Mark and see if I can loosen you up."

Georgia pours some cider into Marks can of Hoffmeister larger.

"Snakebite,"

John is stood in the corner trying to make his cider last, while still using smoke and mirrors to give the illusion he is a seasoned drinker. Emily walks over to him and he smiles awkwardly.

"Hi there and you are?"

"John, I think I remember you from Forchester."

"It seems like forever ago. I suppose, it's kind of large, good chunk of our life, when you are only 16."

John thought this was an intellectual and reflective answer, which raised Emily's stock in his estimations.

"I like the music."

Emily looked puzzled at this remark, surely it was just what every 80's teenager would be listening to. John was no ordinary 80's teenager. His strict up bringing meant he rarely listened to main stream pop music. As soon as "Like a virgin or I want your sex" was heard in the house James would turn it off.

"Do you want some more cider John?"

John took a couple of big gulps to try and empty his mainly still full paper cup.

"Yer, go on mate."

"You're knocking that cider down pretty quickly."

John leans forward to whisper into Emily's ear. He can smell the sweet tones of her perfume.

"In truth I don't really like it, I am only drinking to fit it."

Emily gives John a puzzled look.

"Then why drink it? I don't really like drinking either."

John and Emily smile at each other, all be it slightly awkwardly.

"Do you want to dance John?"

"I don't really dance either."

Emily grabs John by the arm and drags him across the kitchen and into the living room to dance. John takes his first few tentative steps. He appears to have mastered dad dancing, way before it should have kicked in naturally. To his credit he begins to loosen up and gets into a more acceptable dance pattern. The evening passes by quite quickly, as all things enjoyable tend to do. Mr and Mrs Ibbotson's cab can be seen from the lounge window. This was the que for the drink to be put away and the music turned down. Georgia was handing out a packet of Polo mints in a vain attempt to mask the smell of alcohol on the teenager's breath.

The next morning John wakes up with a hangover. He hadn't really drunk before and had zero tolerance to one of the vices of adult life. Several hours later after an assault of water and aspirin he begins to feel better. He had enjoyed having the opportunity to be a real teenager, rather than his father's version of one. This was also his first exposure to having a fun time with the opposite sex. Over the next few weeks he hoped he would bump into Emily. His shyness had prevented him from daring to ask for her phone number. Perhaps even if he had got it, he wouldn't have the bravery required to ring her. Instead he tries to remember the alluring tones of her perfume as he whispered in her ear. The next few months passed by and John was under pressure from his father to make decisions in respect of his education. James wanted John to go to a Church college and eventually into some kind of religion based occupation. John was pretty much done with religion. In his mind directly or indirectly it had contributed to his mother's untimely death.

"John I want you to go to St Pauls College, I have pulled a few strings and they will accept you without your GCSE RE, in consideration of the circumstances."

"Dad I don't want to go to St Pauls. I don't want to be a clergyman, RE teacher or anything else to do with the church."

"Your ungrateful, after all I have done for you."

John had never really given his dad back chat or dared to disagree with him. He had held back his anger since his mother's death. But now he could feel the rage growing within him.

"Dad this is my life not yours. I want to go to College in Nocton with my friends."

"Friends won't get you an education or a career."

"Friends will let me have a happy fulfilled life!"

"Well we will have to agree to disagree. Here is a list of things you need for St Pauls."

"What part of I am not going to St Pauls do you not understand!"

"You are going and that is it""

"I won't let you terrorise me like you did my mother."

"I loved your mother and treated her well."

"If that's the case dad, then why did mum ask you for a divorce three times in the months before her death?"

James is shocked. How did John know about his mum's unhappiness?

"What makes you say that? I don't know what you think you know but it's not true."

"I know, because mum told me! She left a suicide note, which told me all about how unhappy she was and that she wanted a divorce to get away from you. You refused by quoting the marriage vows to her."

"When you take the marriage vows son, it is forever. Until death do we part?"

"It's a load of crap dad. Why would God want people to be unhappy?"

John walks out and slams the door behind him.

James was a stubborn man with his own agenda. His self-centred approach and obsession with the church had already cost him his wife. He wasn't about to completely alienate his son and risk losing him.

John eventually got his own way and was all set to start Business studies at Nocton College. Gone was the craziness of the yellow blazer and purple cap, in favour of whatever you fancied. John wasn't really sure if any of his friends would be going to Nocton. He just knew chances they were was higher than St Pauls. It felt so liberating to have defied his father and to have avoided yet another clash with fashion.

Johns first morning brought the best possible news. He had looked around the class in an attempt to notice a friend. Sat quietly at the back was the very person he had longed to see since the party. Emily was a sight for sore eyes, dressed in high wasted jeans and a pink T shirt. Her hair was big and curly and her eyes a beautiful emerald green. John was filled with a fuzzy warmness inside and he smiled to himself. Emily had spotted John and had given him a beaming smile and mouthed a "Hello."

The morning passed quickly and it was dinner time. John made his way to the canteen with Emily.

"I was hoping I would run into you before today. I enjoyed talking at the party."

"You should have asked for my phone number silly"

"Right, I won't make that mistake again."

John hastily feels in his bag for his diary and a pen.

"Ok fire away."

"Forchester 232687."

John writes down the number followed by Emily in capital letters and a big exclamation mark. John and Emily spend dinner together chatting.

The first week at Nocton was amazing for John not only had he met Emily, but he had enjoyed college. Gone was the prim and proper, stern tutorage of Perthwaite. In its place was the guidance and mentoring of a much younger tutor, who had a connection with his students. There was laughing in class, the occasional joke and a large helping of banter.

It was now the weekend and John was pondering on whether or not to ring Emily. He wanted to but was scared his call might be rebuffed by her parents.

It was now 11am on Saturday morning and John knew if he was to catch Emily in, now was probably the best time to ring. He takes a deep breath and dials. The seconds until the phone is picked up feels like an eternity. Eventually he can hear the receiver being lifted and he takes a deep breath.

"Hello."

An adult male voice replies. "Hello how can I help you?"

"Hello, Its John I go to college with Emily. Is she in?"

"Oh John, Emily has done nothing but talk about you all week. I think I know your dad he's a vicar isn't he. I think he married us. Well I mean we married each other but he conducted the ceremony."

Emily's dads little joke was completely wasted on john.

"Hello."

"I was a bit scared when your dad came on the phone."

"There is no need to be, my mum and dad are great."

"Do you fancy meeting up today at some point?"

"I would love to. What about meeting at the park near the war memorial in half an hour?"

"Brilliant. I want to carry on talking Emily but I would rather get ready and talk face to face."

"Ok, I will see you soon."

John quickly showers and walks into his dad's room to borrow some Brute aftershave. He gets dressed and makes his way to the park. It's a crisp cold day, but sunny.

As he approaches the war memorial he can see Emily in the distance, rubbing her hands together to keep out the cold.

"Hi, John its cold."

"It certainly is Emily."

"Do you want to go for a coffee at the café? My shout."

"Oh I do like an independent women," John jokes.

"I wouldn't say independent. More my dad left me a fiver this morning."

The pair walk off towards the café. Emily wraps her arm around Johns and pulls herself closer to him to keep warm. Such is the level of John's shyness he is blushing. Luckily his embarrassment is masked by his already rosy cheeks.

"What do you want?"

"Just a coffee would be wonderful."

John takes a seat while Emily pays. Five minutes later a waitress brings over two coffees and chip butties.

"Excuse me. We didn't order these."

"No you didn't. The café has been dead all day. To me, you both look cold and hungry and it wouldn't do for young love to be halted by malnutrition."

"Oh we aren't together, we are just friends."

"It's a start young man."

Johns blushing goes into overdrive. Emily plants a kiss on John's cheek and smiles. John feeling ever uncomfortable in the moment changes the conversation.

"Chip butty. Which sauce brown or red?"

"Red every time, but defo brown on bacon."

The waitress over hears the conversation and chips in with. "You see that's a good sign your compatible."

There was nothing more John wanted in the world at that moment than to have Emily has his girlfriend. Now was not the time though. Emily and John soon made short work of the chip butties and coffee. They were contemplating ordering another coffee. Anything to keep out the cold. They spent the next hour dragging out their coffee drinking. Not that the waitress could care less.

Eventually it was time to go and they walked together until they got to the park.

"Emily."

"Yes John."

John pauses for a moment in a period of deep refection.

"Will you?"

Once again he pauses.

"Will I what?"

"Will you do me the honour of being my girlfriend?"

"Only if you can manage to ask me a little less formerly."

"Do you fancy going out together as boyfriend and girlfriend?"

"You know what I would love to. You are so nice. Much better than some of the sleazy lads I went to school with."

"I need to go. So we will see each other soon wont we."

Emily leans forward and this time kisses John square on the lips.

John can feel the butterfly fluttering thing inside and he is full of the warm contentment of young love. The next few weeks went by and John and Emily saw each other at college and home. John had fumbled his way through some French kissing and to his credit he only managed to bite Emily's lip just the once. To say John was smitten was an underestimation. These were the happiest days of his young life. Emily was however keeping a secret from John, her dad had secured a job as a Chief engineer on a contract in the USA. This meant all the family would have to move to the states. Emily was finding it hard to break John's heart. She was very fond of him. Fond to the point it could be love. Having never really experienced the love you feel for a boy or girlfriend, she couldn't be sure.

Going to the USA was a massive opportunity for her too and she felt torn. Every time she tried to approach the subject, she froze. There was now literally a couple of weeks left before the family would fly to North Carolina. John called the house and for once Emily answered.

"Hi what are you up to?"

"I have just been helping mum wash up."

In reality she had been sorting out things in her room and was slow time packing for the states.

"Have you seen the poster on the notice board at Nocton for the Bonfire ball?"

"I can't say I have it sounds great."

Emily knows too well she will be in North Carolina by then. Overcome by guilt and a sudden desire to throw out the dirty washing she begins to tell John.

"John I have something to tell you."

John can detect the stress in her voice and braces himself for bad news.

"John I won't be seeing you again after next week."

"Why is there someone else? Did you meet someone at college? Am I too boring for you?"

"No John, I love you very much. My dad's got a job in America and we are moving out there soon. I have been dreading telling you. I am heartbroken at the thought of not seeing you."

John's world had just fallen apart for the second time in five months.

"I need to go, goodbye Emily I don't think I can bare to meet up or speak any longer. Have a wonderful life. You never know maybe one day."

"Goodbye John. I love you."

John slams the receiver down and begins to cry. He suddenly felt so helpless and lonely in the big adolescent world. Emily did not go to College for the next few weeks. Nocton was never the same for

John after Emily left. Every nook and cranny felt haunted by the presence of her spectre.

John wakes up and reaches for his iPhone. He checks out the time. The display reads 0730am Monday 22nd May 2009. The now 34 year old John was going to be late for work again. For all his qualifications and the Nocton Business diploma, he was working has a parts advisor in a car dealership. He is living alone in a small two bedroom apartment in Nocton. John's dad had died of a heart attack at the age of 58. He had left everything to his only child. John owned his apartment and despite his poor job was comfortable.

John is still fixing his tie, when he sets off in his Ford Fiesta. He had bought it from Brookes, which was the Ford dealers he works at. John pulls into work at 8.14 and is just a little late. Andrew Brooke the Dealer Principle gives John a scowl and looks at his watch. Andrew was in his early 40s had jet black gelled back hair and was a smarmy bastard. The kind of guy you would love to punch on any given day. John enters the parts department.

"Afternoon John."

"Yes I get the point, sorry I am late."

"Don't let it happen again. At least until next time."

John's supervisor, Richard was ex- military and didn't really take life too seriously. The importance of car parts always seemed trivial compared to the provision of weapons to the front lines during his days in Logistics Corp.

"Did you have a good weekend Rich?"

"Brilliant mate, I went to a reunion with the lads from the Corp."

"Where did you go?"

"Blackpool mate. Drank too much, chewed the fat and met some tricky birds."

"Met some tricky birds?"

"Sorry mate I will translate. Good looking and up for it."

"Good one mate."

John actually felt a bit repulsed by Richards's behaviour. Richard was married with two kids in their early teens. If he had a girl he would never cheat on her.

One of the salesmen enters the stores.

"Have you monkeys got that new key yet for that orange Focus ST?" Oh yer, I forgot Rich, the only ST you have is an STD."

"Fuck off Dave. Do you know what Dave, you could be a comedian if it wasn't for just one thing."

"What that?"

"You are not fucking funny!"

Chapter 4
Just an ordinary girl

Apart from Andrew and the occasional dick of a salesman the job was ok, but nothing more. Without his dad or a partner in life John lacked motivation. The day's work was done and John was sat at home eating a prawn linguini microwave meal for one and drinking a glass of Pinot. He was thinking back to his first encounter with alcohol at the party in 1989. He became somewhat melancholy as he recalled the wonderful times he had with Emily and wondered what she was doing now. I guess there is a fair chance that many people remember their first love and perhaps what could have been. John watches the usual bland nonsense on TV before the drink takes it toil and he begins to feel tired.

The following morning John had no waking up issues and was eating cereals while watching TV. The morning TV programme was interrupted by the local news.

"In local news. Police are concerned for a local man named Mark Smith age 29. He has been missing for the past three weeks after a night out with friends in Nocton. He was last seen on CCTV coming out of a bar on Sandygate. Police are keen to hear from anybody who may have come into contact with Mark on the night of Saturday 1st May or have seen him since."

Nocton wasn't really the kind of place where people go missing. Then again Hungerford wasn't really the kind of place where people get shot. John finished off his coffee and went to work.

"Did you see the news this morning about that guy who's been missing three weeks, after a night out in Nocton?"

"Strange mate."

"I know him. We used to play football together a few years ago. He was probably off his tits and went for a walk down by the canal. He was a massive coke head and always got smashed."

"Well whatever he was into I hope he is ok."

"Anything can happen to anybody anywhere if you don't keep your wits about you."

"Says the highly trained ex-Special Forces operator."

"You couldn't pass the fitness test for the Salvation army."

John loved all the work banter. He tried to join in whenever possible but lacked the sarcasm and sharpness of thought.

On the outskirts of Nocton, Andrea Walker is in the back garden of her sprawling 1830s detached cottage. Which is complete with an old blacksmiths shop and furnace. She is cleaning ashes from the furnace. To be more specific, she is cleaning the ashes of Mark Smith from the furnace. Andrea is in her mid-30s and has strawberry blonde hair and beautiful green eyes. A girl who oozes class but still has a cheeky flirty side. She is the kind of person men want to be with and women aspire to be like. Andrea works as a nursey nurse at Big World nursery. She is polite and speaks with a soft Southern Irish accent. Serial killers come in all shapes and sizes. She disposes of the ashes by mixing them amongst compost at the bottom of the garden. Having completed her grizzly task she makes herself a drink and sits down to watch TV.

The next morning, Andrea is walking the two miles to work. It's a beautiful day and she can feel the sun on her face. Her green eyes are framed by a pair of blue lensed Ray Ban aviators.

Big world has a pink and yellow wooden picket fence with a number of scenes from around the world on the outside of the building. Things such as the jungles of Africa, Nepalese mountains and the New York skyline.

There are already a number of small children in the nursery playground.

"Good morning Miss Walker."

Andrea looks down to see a little blonde-haired girl with pink glasses and a snotty nose looking up at her.

"Good morning sweetie."

The little girls mum wipes her nose and kisses her.

"I will take her in for you."

"You are so lucky to have Miss Walker as your teacher, she is lovely."

Andrea smiles and takes the little girl by the hand and leads her into the nursery.

"Good morning Andrea"

"Good morning Maggie"

Did you see all the police and PCSO's in town this morning?

"Why! What's happened?

"I think they are doing some enquiries into that missing man that disappeared a few weeks ago."

Andrea doesn't miss a beat, she shrugs her shoulders and looks concerned. "That's awful, I hope they find him soon. I bet his family are worried sick."

The conversation is halted by a boy in the corner of the room who was crying for his mum and trying to fight his way out of the door.

Miss Andrea Walker had lived in the town all her life. She had inherited her cottage from her parents, who died in a boating accident whilst on holiday four years ago. Her interests beyond murder were keeping fit and writing poetry. To the outside world she was a lovely, intellectual young women, who lived a fulfilling life.

John was leaving work for the weekend and was making his way to the car.

"Hey John, what are you up to this weekend?"

"Not a great deal mate, TV, takeaway, beer, sleep."

"Do you fancy going out into town for a few beers tomorrow night?"

John pauses for a moment and considers his options.

"Love to mate. What time?"

"I was going to catch a cab into town at about 8pm. I will swing by yours and pick you up not long after."

John drives off, half wishing he hadn't bothered acquiescing to Richards's suggestion. Any kind of social interaction in a busy setting wasn't really John's thing. The next morning John was reading an article on being confident on the internet. The article suggested, if you look the part, you feel the part. With this in mind, John decided to put his best foot forward and go into town to buy some new clothes. Nocton town centre wasn't exactly a sprawling mecca for high end fashion. John spent the first hour or two looking around the mainstreamers like Next, Topman and Burton. Nothing seemed to take his fancy. Everything was just much of a muchness. Eventually John came across a small independent shop. After perusing the window for a short while he goes in. Fifteen minutes later he comes out with a pair of Tommy Hilfiger chinos and a blue short sleeved Ralph Lauren shirt. He was also £150 lighter in the pocket. The walk to the car takes him passed Costa coffee. He can see two women sat in the window. One is in her mid-40s with a curly brunette bob. The other in her early to mid-30s, with strawberry blonde hair and green eyes. She stands up and walks towards the door.

Chapter 5
Smoke and mirrors

Seconds later she appears wearing a pair of blue lensed aviators. John continues walking towards his car.

"Shit, I have left my phone in Costa Andrea!"
"You have got a head like Jelly."
"That's me,"
"Go on give it a wobble."

Maggie retrieves her phone and breathes a sigh of relief.

"Right let's get some serious shopping done. I have got my credit card so I might treat you."
Andrea was generous and would think nothing of spending money on her friends.

"We had best save some money for tonight, those shots won't buy themselves."

It is now a quarter past 7 and John is getting into the shower. He steps in and straight back out again, because the water was still cold. After a few minutes of playing with the controls the water was getting no warmer. He takes a deep breath and jumps in. He picks up the scrunchie and pours shower jell over it to create a foam. He quickly washes his body and stays under the streams of cold water just long enough for the foam to wash away. As he steps out of the shower he begins to shiver. He hopes the rest of the evening will go somewhat better.

Over at the cottage Andrea has hung outfits all over her bedroom on the handles of her built in wardrobes. She is pondering over the nights outfit. Will it be a dress, jeans and a slinky top or something super sexy? Dressing to kill literally, was not an option most predators get.

Eventually she settles for a pair of tight faded jeans and a backless black top. She slips on her earrings and sprays Miss Dior on her neck and wrists just as the doorbell rings.
"Come in!"
Andrea makes her way down the stairs and meets Maggie in the hallway.
"Wow look at you Miss Walker you look amazing."
"You don't look too shabby yourself Mags."
"You know how they say you can't polish a turd. Well it appears you can."
"Give over. You are lovely for an older women."
"Typical of you Andrea. What you give with one hand you take back with the other."
"That's why you love me."
"Sure do."

John fresh from polar expedition is checking out his new outfit in the mirror. He is more than happy with his new look and smiles to himself. Ten minutes later he is in the cab with Richard heading for the bars of Sandygate. The cab stops outside the Totem bar which is their first port of call.

"What you having pal?"
"Just a beer."
"Fuck that. Two mojitos mate."
The mojitos arrive in tall glasses with a sprig of mint like a small privet hedge.
"What do you think mate?"
"Bloody strong."
It is only 8.30 pm and the bar is still quiet. There are a couple of groups who appear to have come out straight from work.

Thirty minutes later, Rich and John make their way into Zampos. Zampos is a trendy wine bar with an upbeat vibe and was the place to be. Rich walks in first and checks out the clientele. The place is crammed with groups of thirty something ladies.
Rich uses the Maverick line from Topgun.
"This looks like a target rich environment."
"What do you mean?" John says naively,
"Lots of women mate."
The Mojitos are now binned in favour of bottles of Bud. The primary reason being the £9 price tag.

Andrea and Mags are downing another Champagne cocktail in the bar across the road from Zampos.
Mags feels a tap on her shoulder. She looks round to see a slightly chubby man in his 40s. He is

wearing a shirt with the top three buttons undone. Close by is another much slimmer man with teeth that would be at home on the Jeremy Kyle show.
"Hi love can I buy you a drink?"
"Do you think these two are worth turning for darling?"
Andrea gently pulls Maggie towards her by the back of the neck and kisses her softly on the lips.
"Sorry boys we aren't really into guys."
"I would still love that drink though."
The two guys walks off and the girls giggle to themselves.
"That was hilarious."
"By the way your lipstick tasted great."
"Be careful you really are turning."
"Have you ever?"
"Do you want the truth?"
"Of course."
"Well yes the once."
"Never."
"So are you bi or gay."
"No way. It was just a pissed incident. I was on holiday and met this Italian model. We got very drunk and one thing lead to another."
"Miss Walker, I have seen you in a different light now."

If only Maggie knew Andreas real deepest secrets.

John was just a little drunk. In the state where inhibitions drop and you are feeling good but not too drunk?

"Let's go speak to some ladies mate."
John's Dutch courage levels were quite high now and he was up for it.
"Ok mate you take the lead."
They walk over to a couple of women in their mid to late 30's. Richard checks out their wedding rings and he diverts his attentions to a pair of blondes sat on stools near the bar.

"Hi ladies are you having a good night?"
"Yes it's been great apart from those two guys over there who keep hitting on us."
One of the girls points to a couple of guys sat near the other side of the bar. One is in his mid-40s and chubby with a shirt undone like he was Tony Moreno in Saturday night fever. The other was much thinner. They were the same pair who had approached Maggie and Andrea.

"Ok we will be you guardian angels. This is John, he is new to Nocton and I am showing him around."
The girls introduce themselves as Louise and Faye.

John sits next to Faye and leans in a little closer to talk. The music in the bar was just at a volume were you could hear each other if you shouted or moved closer.
"What are you drinking Faye?"
"It's a Cuba Libra,"
"What's that?"
"It's a fancy name for rum and coke."
"Do you want another?"

"Not just yet. I am too busy talking to you."
"What do you do when you are not in bars trying to avoid being hit on?"
"I am a hairdresser."
"I work at a car dealership. But don't worry I am not a salesman. You won't talk to me then suddenly think you feel the need to change your car"
"I can guarantee that won't happen, for the simple reason I don't drive."
They both laugh
"I tell you what my little hero, you can buy me that Cuba Libra now."
"I would love to."

John wondered off to the bar which was stacked three deep with customers.

He returns to the table fifteen minutes later. Faye is on her own. Richard and Louise are talking on another table. He feels a little uncomfortable for Faye who is just staring into space and waiting.

"Sorry about that the bar is rammed."
"No worries, they have wondered off to talk. Without you here I felt like a gooseberry."
"Well I am back now."

They both look over at Richard and Louise. Richard is tapping Louise's mobile number into his phone. No doubt she will be under the name of Lewis in case his wife interrogates his phone.

"Can I have your number?"
"Yer, sure."

John takes out his mobile and Faye taps the number in. Could this be the new Emily? In John's mind there might never be a new Emily.

Both couples continue talking for the next half hour. Louise walks over.

"I really need to think about getting home Faye. Work calls in the morning and I don't want to get carried away."

Richard whispers in John's ear.

"I wish she would."

The boys give Louise and Faye a hug and a continental kiss on both cheeks.

They say their goodbyes and the girls leave.

"Success mate. I noticed you got Faye's number."

"She seems nice."

"If you mean great tits and a fine arse then yer."

John finally gets home at 2.30am and staggers through his front door. To his credit he manages to take off his new clothes and hangs them up. As soon as his head hits the pillow the room starts to spin. John shuts his eyes and tries to fall asleep. Eventually he springs up off the bed with his hand over his mouth in a vain attempt at keeping vomit from the floor. The very moment his head reaches the toilet bowl, the tide of sick cascades from his mouth.

The next morning John wakes up feeling like he will surely die. He thinks to himself. There appears to be a pattern forming here. Go out-meet a nice girl-wake up feeling shit.

By mid-afternoon, John feels better and decides to try ring Faye. He presses the call button but the number will not go through. He tries a number of times. He thinks to himself, typical I must have copied the number down wrong.

Moments later he receives a text from Rich.

"That bird from last night has given me a hooky number."

He replies, "Yes me too. I guess they were playing us for drinks."

Andrea is in Mrs Timbwells garden helping out. Mrs Timbwell is her 87 year old neighbour. Since her husband's death six months earlier, the garden had reached a state of disarray. Walking with the aid of a Zimmer frame, she could do very little about it. Andrea was keen to show a willingness to help anybody. Perhaps it was the alter ego of the monster inside her.

"I think you might need some compost to plant those new rose trees dear."

"It's ok Doreen, I have brought some of my own from next door."

At least Marks final resting place would be marked by the grandeur of some beautiful rose bushes. There was also the convenience of disposing of key evidence. It takes couple of hours for Andrea to finish her tasks.

"I am done Doreen."

Doreen tries to thrust a twenty pound note into Andrea's hand.

"Don't be silly, you hold onto your money Doreen. It was a pleasure to help."

"I am so happy to have you has a neighbour, you are such a sweetheart. The kids at school must love you."
"I would hope they do. Let me know when you need some more gardening doing. I might need some more compost."
"It's ok I will get you some. "
"Don't worry I only use special stuff on your garden Doreen."

Monday morning arrives and John and Richard are reflecting on the night out.
"I can't believe them girls did us over like a kipper with the phoney mobile numbers."
"It's all a game mate, for every one you win you lose ten."
"Only another 9 before success then Rich."
"You seemed to be doing ok with Faye too mate."
"She was nice. I think the booze was doing most of the talking."
"It's that sweet spot, when you are not totally drunk but bristling with confidence."
The parts office door opens and a young Salesman walks in.
"Andrew wants everybody in the showroom now."
They walk through and Andrew gives his brief.

"As you may or may not be aware a young man called Mark Smith disappeared a few weeks ago after a night out in Nocton. A police search team will be coming on site in the morning to check out the perimeter of the pitch and the storage compound. I want four volunteers to have a look first. It would be highly embarrassing if the police found a body on the premises that we haven't noticed.

Andrea returns from Big Worlds with a banging headache. It had been a very difficult day, with nursery staff and kids alike having meltdowns.

She makes her way upstairs to her bedroom and lays down. After an hour of rest with no sleep, she reaches under a pillow and pulls out a 5"locking knife with a serrated edge. This was the weapon she had used to kill Mark Smith. During love making she had taken the opportunity to slit his throat. The mattress is protected from blood by two water proof liners. Under the bed is a 5kg bag of Fullers earth. This is a substance with absorbent qualities, absolutely nothing was left to chance. For the next five minutes she sits on the edge of the bed opening and closing the knife before returning it to its place under the pillow. Her thoughts, now change to selecting her next victim. For serial killers, murder is a drug which releases a rush of euphoria at the point death is inflicted. Andrea Walker was ready for her next fix. Somewhere out there in Nocton or far beyond was the unsuspecting next victim. It was now just a matter of identifying that victim and luring him to his death.

Over in a nearby village on the outskirts of Nocton, Daniel Bates a 29 year old single self-employed electrician is say eating yet another takeaway. It was either that or yet another meal for one. He has been single for the last 8 months and it was mow time to get back on the horse. Daniel was a good looking man with wavy blonde hair and a well-groomed stubble. His desire to find the girl of his dreams would be his downfall.

John was also contemplating getting on the dating scene, but didn't want to go down the line of on line dating. He wanted to meet the one in a more organic way. The sands of time weren't exactly running out for him, but if he wanted to meet a girl and have a family it would be better sooner than later. Even though 19 years had passed by, John still judged all females by the values he has seen many years ago in Emily.

It was Friday night and Andrea was in her car on the way to a pub on the road leading from Nocton to Forchester. She knew that it was a watering hole for men wanting a couple of drinks after a hard working week. More importantly it was fairly secluded and had no CCTV. The everyday Andrea was a kind, thoughtful beautiful individual. The evil alter ego was a cold calculated bitch. She drives passed the pub a number of times, to check out who might be there. On her third pass she pulls into the carpark. She leaves her red Mini Cooper under a tree out of the way of a number of rep mobiles and works vans. She weaves through the vans on the way to the front door. She stops by the side of a small Green Peugeot Partner van and takes a screw driver from her bag. She drops a lip stick to the floor from her bag. As she bends down to pick it up, she drives the screwdriver into the tyre. She smiles and carries on walking to the door. She walks past the tables full of workmen supping their pints and goes straight to the bar. She does not order a drink, but instead tells the bar staff there is a van outside with a flat tyre and gives the registration number. The member of staff asks for silence and announces Andrea's news to the pubs customers. A Blonde haired man in his early 30's puts down his drink and leaves the pub. Andrea follows him out to the carpark.

"Oh hi. I just parked my car up and noticed you have a flat tyre."
"It seemed OK when I parked up."
"It looks like somebody has stabbed it with something, I noticed a couple of youths walking away from the carpark as I arrived."
"Little bastards."
"I bet you are gutted, let me buy you a drink."
"In my world men buy ladies drinks."
"No worries I am parched."
"My names Daniel by the way, but you can call me Dan."
"Pleased to meet you Daniel, my names Andrea."
Andrea and Daniel work back into the pub and go to the bar.
"What's your poison? "
"A red wine, would be more than lovely."
"Red wine and a larger please love."
"That's £10.60 please."
Dan puts his bank card to the terminal and pays.

"Cheers."
Dan and Andrea sit in a corner away from the drinking workforce.

Chapter 6
Daniels driving

"It's not what you need when you finish work for the week."
"After we have had this drink, I will go and change my tyre."
"Do you live locally?"
"Yes not far away, I am a self-employed electrician and rely on the van for work."
"I don't think these stupid youths think about stuff like that. Maybe one day when they are older the penny might drop."
"I don't mean to be too forward and I know we have just met, do you have a boyfriend or are you single?"
"Who said it had to be a boyfriend."
Daniel feels embarrassed.
"Oh I am sorry I didn't think."
"No if I had a partner it would be a boy, I was just pulling your leg."
Daniel likes a girl with a sense of humour. The remark endeared Andrea to him even more."
"How do you fancy meeting here tomorrow for a drink during the day?"
"You know what, you seem like such a nice guy I would love to."
"I will leave the van at home tomorrow though I will probably have a couple and still drive."
"So what do you drive when you are not working?"

"I have an Audi S3."
"Oh an Audi is it fast?"
Andrea is a car fan and knows very well what Dan's car is capable of. She was just acting the innocent naïve blonde.
"Shall we say meet at about 2?"
"I will look forward to it."
Daniel and Andrea drink up and say their goodbyes.

Andrea feels satisfied at the thought of once again being on the road to starting up the furnace in the old Blacksmiths shop. Andrea in turn was totally Daniels cup of tea and he hoped the chance meeting might lead to more.

John is at work and has wondered through into the showroom to look at the new Ford Focus ST in bright orange. To be fair it probably wasn't everyone's cup of teas. As he walks around, a salesman, Tony walks over.
"Fancying one Mate?"
"It's nice but probably a little too flash for me."
"I guess you don't get paid fortunes in stores either mate, its nearly 20 grand"
John thought this was a typical cocky salesman thing to say and felt like he was being mocked. In reality John could nip out over lunch and withdraw 20k. Even if he wanted the bright orange Felice, he wouldn't be giving Tony the satisfaction.
"Maybe one day mate."
Tony hadn't completely failed in his job, the seed of changing his car was now firmly planted in Johns

mind. John walks back into the stores and speaks to Richard.
"Tony's just tried to sell me that orange Focus ST."
"Wouldn't have one given mate. I would rather spend 20 grand on a used Audi, Merc or Beamer. You can't beat a German motor. Much better than these things. The RAF won the Battle of Britain because of the pilots, but you can bet the Messerschmitt's were more reliable than the Spitfires."

The following day Andrea is thinking about her date with Daniel. This would not be the day she did the deed, it was merely the beginning of some groundwork. Like the spider locating a suitable location to build the web to catch the fly. Never the less she had a passion for her work and made sure everything was in place, should the situation become more fluid and the opportunity arise. After all Doreen's demand for compost might become more pressing at any given moment.
Andrea as selected a short yellow dress with pink daisies from her wardrobe. It is demure but still alluring. She finishes the look with a faded denim jacket, should the day get chilly."

Daniel is wearing a pair of beige chinos, a light blue denim shirt and loafers minus socks. He looks a little bit like a young Jude Law but with more hair. He fires up the engine of the Audi and drives off. He is happy with the excitement of anticipation. Even though he has only had a fleeting meeting with

Andrea, he felt she was a good candidate for the one. The S3 weaves its way around the winding roads leading to the pub. Inside the car, Daniel is listening to some up beat dance music as the tunes resonate in his head his speed increases. Modern cars install a confidence in their drivers that makes them feel invincible. Take away the electronic stability control, anti-lock brakes and a ditch awaits. When you add the endorphins Daniel is experiencing into the mix his driving goes from confident to damn right reckless. In the distance he can see a tractor just before a right hand bend. He accelerates knowing the S3 can corner like it is on rails. Like any activity with a degree of danger the more danger the more adrenaline is released. Daniels toe presses down a little harder on the accelerator and the S3s velocity is at its maximum capability. He steers right to overtake. As he does he can see just beyond the tractor on his side of the road a broken down lorry. He panics and tries to dive through the gap. The rear nearside wing clips the front of the tractor and the S3 begins to loose traction and spins. Inside the S3 Daniel is fighting with the steering wheel desperately trying to stop the spin. His efforts are all in vain as the S3 collides with the front of the lorry and ends Daniels life.

An hour later Andrea tries to pass the same road having in her mind been stood up by Daniel.
The police stop her and explain there has been a serious accident and the road is blocked.

The following week Andrea is in the kitchen when the local newspaper the Nocton Bugle is dropped through the letter box. She walks over to the hallway to pick it up. As she makes her way back into the kitchen she unfolds it and turns the first page. There is a half-page article entitled "Tragic road death of young Nocton man." Daniel Bates 29 lost his life in a collision with a lorry on the A22 Nocton to Forchester Road. His powerful Audi S3 went into a spin after an overtaking move, said eye witness George Franks who was on the same road driving a tractor. Andrea takes no joy from Daniels awful death. She would now have to start the victim selection process again. She sighs and takes a gulp of coffee.

Over at John's apartment he too is reading the same article. His thoughts turn to the salesman tempting him into buying the Focus ST. He doubts he could be tempted into such reckless behaviour even if he had a fast car. The thought of a car change however was now firmly planted in his mind. Why shouldn't he treat himself to a new car he thought? He worked hard and had the money so he decided he would. Taking into consideration Richards advice he brings up the Website of a dealers in Nocton called. "All German Autos." The first car on the list of stock is an Audi S3. With the memory of Daniels demise still fresh in his mind he scrolls straight past it. There is a mind blowing number of Audi's Mercs and BMWs to choose from.

Eventually a BMW 335d M sport coupe in black takes his eye. 2007 model. 19000 miles, automatic, cream leather seats. One owner from new. £18500.
Feeling in a decisive mood he gets in the hapless Fiesta and makes his way to the dealers.
He pulls onto the forecourt. Right in front of him is the Beemer. He excitedly gets out of the ford and starts to look around. A salesman wearing a blue BMW M Sport polo shirt goes over to speak to him.

"How can I help you?"
"I saw this BMW on your website so I thought I would come and take a look."
"It's only been in a few days. It's a lovely motor. As a salesman there are nice motors and then nice motors you would buy yourself. This is the latter."
John liked that line. This guy was in his fifties and seemed much more genuine than Tony and the sales team at Brookes.
"I will go get you the keys. Oh, come to think of it the keys are in my pocket because I put some new mats in this morning."

Ten minutes later John is adjusting the driver's seat ready for his test drive.
"Right just pull out of the entrance and turn right. It takes us onto the A22 and you can open her up a bit. Right ease off, then slam your foot hard on the gas."
The BMW drops down a gear and catapults forward.
"Wow that moves."

"It certainly does mate. But if you drive like a vicar you still get nearly 50MPG."
John laughs at this remark and recalls his dad plodding along in his Ford Escort.
They pull into the dealers.
"Well do you like the car?"
"It's everything I expected it would be."
"Well if we can get the figures right."
For all John's naivety with women, he was nobody's fool when it came down to money."
Twenty minutes later after some shrewd negotiation he had completed the deal and drove away in his new car.
Johns mum and dad had never been ones for wasting money on pretentious things. For a fleeting moment he felt a slight ting of guilt because of his self-indulgence. He then headed for the open road to enjoy his new purchase.

Mrs Timbwell is talking to Andrea over the garden fence.
"Hello Andrea aren't you working today?"
"It's half term Doreen so I have got a bit of freedom."
"Would you care to come over for a cup of tea?"
"I would love to, but please be careful putting that kettle on."
"I will, if that's an order."
"It certainly is soldier."
As Andrea gets to Doreen's door she can hear the clanging of china.

"Come in love. There's your tea, would you like sugar?"

"No thank you."

"Doreen had prepared tea like it was served at the Savoy. Royal Albert tea cups and saucers complete with paper doilies."

"This is lovely Doreen."

"I always think tea tastes far better in china cups than a grotty pot mug."

Andrea takes a gentle sip from the side of her cup and then puts the cup back on the doily."

"Would you be a darling and fetch that Victoria sponge in from the kitchen side?"

Moments later Andrea returns with the cake, side plates and forks.

"You can be mum."

"Andrea cuts two slices of cake and puts them on the plates. She hands one to Mrs Timbwell.

"So Andrea no sign of any young man in your life yet."

"No not yet. I think they all seem to be into cars, drinking and the gym. I want a man who likes walking in the country, and reading. It would also be great if he was good in the garden."

Andrea smirks to herself over her cryptic garden clue. She never did get to find out if Daniel was good in the garden and neither did Doreen's roses.

"Yes I saw something in the Bugle about a young man dying in a car the other week. It's a shame from the picture I saw he looked. What's that phrase you young people use these days?"

"He looked fit."

"That's the one fit. If I was only ten years younger."
"Oh Doreen I am beginning to see you in a different light."
"I haven't always been old dear, I have had my movements."
"I bet you have Doreen."
For the next hour the sassy old lady recalls stories of her conquests to Andrea.

It's Monday morning and as John pulls into the works car park the BMW doesn't go unnoticed by his peers.
"Nice car mate. You should have come to me I could have got you some cheap payments on the Focus."
"No payments required Tony. Cash is King."
John doesn't even know where he pulled that phrase from. It wasn't something he had ever said before. David Dickinson or Dell Trotter came to mind has a possible source. With Tony firmly put in his place, John continues to walk into the parts department.
"Good morning Rich."
Rich lets out a laboured "Morning."
The next two hours until tea break are shrouded in silence apart from work related communication.
"What's up with you mate? You have hardly said a word all morning."
"She's left me."
"What?"
Rachel's left me and taken our Bethany with her."
"Sorry mate, what happened?"

"I met a bird on line a few weeks ago. Nothing serious just one of those meet and fuck things. Rach was away. Like an idiot I took her back to mine and did her. She must have lost an earring in the bed and when Rach changed the sheets she found it."

"Bloody hell mate, it's been coming."

"To add insult to injury, she went round to Allison's next door. Somehow she realised it must have happened when she was away. Allison's CCTV camera overlooks our front door and it captured me walking in with this lass."

"As you know I am no expert on relationships, but as a ley man I would say you are pretty much fucked."

For all Richards philandering he genuinely loved his wife and worshipped his daughter.

"Where do you think she has gone?"

"Probably to her sisters, she lives on the West coast of Scotland somewhere or other."

"What will you do now?"

"There is not a lot I can do until she contacts me or comes home."

"If you play with fire mate."

"It's official. I am an overactive dick with an over active dick."

Rich does his best to smile.

"Pub tonight for tea mate, my shout."

"I won't see you sat around on your own tonight wondering what to do with yourself."

"Thanks mate I promise not to be so bloody miserable for the rest of the day."

The working day ends with Richards spirits raised just a little. He had fucked up but knew for now there was nothing he could do. If you walk the tightrope long enough you will fall off eventually it's inevitable.

Richard takes seat in the Beamer.
"Great car mate. Like I said you can't beat some German metal."
"It does the trick mate. For a few fleeting seconds John stretches the legs of the Beamer, before settling into a more leisurely pace. They pull into the pub carpark just as a Mini Cooper is pulling out.
John parks the BMW under a tree in the corner of the pub car park. As he gets out he notices something on the floor. He picks it up and shows it to Richard. It's an ID card with a bright yellow lanyard.
"Big Worlds nursery, Miss Andrea Walker."
John tucks the ID into the glove compartment and they both walk into the pub.

Later that evening Andrea is preparing herself for work the next day. Clothes, shoes, clean underwear, car keys, lunch, ID. Make that no ID. She is fairly sure it will be upstairs by her bed, in the bowl near the front door or in the car. As she checks of the locations without success her heart sinks. We all go through that I can't find it but it will be here somewhere phase. Swiftly followed by owe shit, it really is very, very missing. This was the stage Andrea was now at. She had now done all she could to find it. It wasn't like there was a possibility she could have left it at a crime scene.

The next day she reports the matter to the nursery manager.
Literally minutes after doing so, a black BMW pulls up outside the nursery.
John goes up to the gate and speaks to Maggie.
"Hi there I found this in the carpark of a pub."
John's hands over the ID.
"Andrea Walkers ID left in a pub car park. Well there is a surprise!"
"I will take that thank you."
Andreas hand snatches the ID from Maggie.
"I think you had better say thanks to this young man."
John was already halfway out of the nursery gate at this point. He does however look round just long enough to see Andrea. He can't help but think that the ID photo does her no justice. She gives him an electrifying smile. As her head turns her beautiful blonde hair gently wafts against her cheek.
She was quite John's cup of tea and the snap shot in time will remain with him.

"That was a relief Mags. I knew I had lost it last night but finding it was another thing."
"At least getting another descent ID photo would have been easy with your beautiful face. This old mug would need some photo shop."
"Get lost Mags if I was a bloke I would."

"Especially if you was drunk and I was an Italian model."
"Shush!!!Kids."
"Sorry."

Richard was at the back of the dealership talking to Rachel. Out of the way of prying eyes and ears.
"I want a divorce you prick."
"Rach how can I argue with you. I have been a complete dickhead."
"She's not the only one is she?"
Richard is like a rabbit in the headlights and just stays silent.
"Your silence speaks volumes Rich."
"All I ask is you don't drag Bethany into things."
"She knows how her dads a dirty bastard."
Richards's eyes fill with tears. He loves Bethany and would never want to hurt her. In truth Richards's marriage had died a death many years ago. The only thing that kept them together was finances, familiarity and Bethany. There was no real love, intimacy or mutual respect.
"What are you going to do now?"
"I am staying up here with Jody for a while until I figure out what to do."

Chapter 7
A lamb to the slaughter

"Please tell Bethany I will ring her tonight and tell her I love her."
The phone goes dead. Richard tries to compose himself before going back into work.
"Are you ok mate?"
"I have just spoken to Rach. It's a fucking nightmare mate."
"You really have done it this time."
"I am going to lose everything mate, the house, Rach, Beth and my fucking sanity."
Rich throws his cup at the wall and instantly feels regret. It was a father's day present from Beth and the message on it read. "The world's greatest dad with me always." But it wasn't true was it Beth was 400 miles away in another country. Richard begins to full on cry. He was in the age group where showing your emotions in such a way still feels awkward and alien. John puts a reassuring hand on Richards's shoulder, before wiping the wall and picking up the broken mug. For a moment John thinks that maybe relationships are worth avoiding.

Andrea arrives back home at 4.30 and sits down with a green tea flicking through Facebook.
She has received a message request. She clicks accept and see's the message is from a guy called Matthew.

"I hope you don't think I am being too forward but I saw your picture on Facebook and thought wow, she is amazing."

Andrea thinks for a moment and then starts to type.

"I find your direct approach quite refreshing."

Andrea checks out Mathews profile whilst she awaits a reply. He is only 22 which is a bit young. But hey, if he doesn't mind being mauled by the cougar. Maybe his naivety will make him easier to lower into her lair. A full hour later her phone finally pings.

"Hello Andrea pleased to meet you. Can we chat?"

"I would love to. Here's my mobile number message me on here. 07368650521."

The mobile number was a burner phone.

"Thanks for the number. I know you are a little older than me but I like older women. All the ones my age are into lip fillers and reality TV. I want the company of a real women. "

Andrea instantly ages 10 years in her mind.

"So Mat. What do you like about me apart from my age?"

"I think your hair is amazing and your eyes are beautiful."

"Is there anything else you like about my body?"

"You are making me feel all hot and bothered now."

"That was the idea Matthew."

Andrea mirrors Matthews's direct approach and sends over a picture in her underwear.

"Do you like what you see?"

Matthew is taken aback by the picture and how forward Andrea was now being. It was all part of her plan. She had, a number of intimate pictures on her burner phone for exactly this kind of eventuality. In the world of the serial killer anything goes. Andrea knew that over sexualising herself was the best way to snare a younger man.

"You are gorgeous."

"This is your reward for being a brave boy."

"Boy. I am a man."

"Show me!"

A few minutes later Andrea receives the standard cock shot.

"Nice! Gives me something to work with."

"Do you want to meet up?"

Bingo! Andrea's faith in human nature had rewarded her with an opportunity.

"Where do you live?"

"Marsden Heath."

By chance Marsden Heath was only about 30 miles away.

"Meet me at the, Old twisted Monk on the A22 near Forchester. "

"When."

"If you want me like I think you do now."

Mat can't believe that a random message to a girl he didn't know could lead to a nailed on fuck.

"I will meet you at 7.30."

"I am wet just thinking about it."

Andrea throws on a short denim dress and reaches for a strapless bra. Knickers weren't required. Before she leaves she checks the lock knife is in place.

Andrea pulls her Mini into the carpark of the pub at a little after 7.40. There are only three other cars in the car park. One of which is occupied by Mat. Andrea walks over to the passenger side of Mats Honda Civic and opens the door.
"Matthew."
"Yes."

She leans in and puts her hand on the crotch of Mats jeans. She then steps out of her car and beckons him over to her Mini. They both get in and Andrea sits with her dress hitched up and her legs slightly apart. Mat goes to kiss her and she pushes him away.
"Don't be too anxious we have got all night."
They both sit in silence during the 15 minute journey. Mat is finding it hard to hide his excitement.
As they go through the door of the cottage they begin to kiss and Andrea wraps her legs around him.
"Carry me too the bedroom and do with me what you will."

Mat follows her request and they both fall onto the bed. Mat takes his time to undo the buttons on Andreas dress before unclipping her bra. Andrea is pulling on Mats belt. He caresses her breast in his hands and kisses her nipples before, making his way down her body with his mouth. As he kisses the inside of her thigh she reaches under the pillow for the locking knife. Finally locating the button that extends the blade. She slides the knife out from under the pillow. She closes her legs forcing Mat to look up. As he does she runs the serrated blade across his neck. He immediately grabs his neck to stop the flow of blood. He begins to make a gargling sound as the blood flows from the wound and into his windpipe. Eventually he succumbs to his injury and dies. The blood is pooling on the bed and starting to flow close to the sides of the mattress. Andrea reaches under the bed and throws handfuls of Fullers earth around to soak it up. She then bends over and kisses Mat on the lips before wiping the blood from her face. She showers and goes downstairs leaving Mats lifeless body on her bed.

It's now 3am. Andrea looks out of her windows front and back to see if her neighbour's lights are on. She assumes they are all in bed and the coast is clear .Andrea untucks the sheets and mattress covers from her bed and wraps them around the body, before binding them with a thin cord. She throws an old quilt over the first few steps and slides Mats body onto it before using it to slide him down the stairs. Even with the aid of the old quilt it is still hard work. Andrea can feel perspiration coming from her head and her back is soaked. She wheels a barrow to the back door and struggles to lift Mat onto it. Eventually she manages to push the rickety old wheel barrow to the Blacksmiths shop at the bottom of the garden. By the morning Matthews remains are ready to be composted.

It's now 8.30 am and Andrea is leaving for work. Doreen is in the garden putting some seed out for the birds.

"Morning! You look tired Andrea."
"I had a bit of a heavy night Doreen."
"Burning the candle at both ends."
"I don't even own a candle."
"I don't mean to be rude, but I am a bit late for work Doreen."
"Oh Sorry love, I will catch you later."
"Bye,"
Doreen lucked disappointed that Andrea didn't have time to talk. This didn't go unnoticed by Andrea. She smiles to herself as she gets a light bulb moment.
It's now mid-morning and Doreen is watching Lorraine Kelly on ITV, when the doorbell rings.
She stands up slowly, not without some considerable pain to her right hip. The doorbell rings again.
"I am coming."
She opens the door to see a delivery driver stood on her front door step. Behind him parked on the road she can see a Transit van with the words, Lloyds Garden Centre on the side.
"Are you Mrs Doreen Timbwell?"
"Yes that's right."
"I have a delivery for you."
"Are you sure I am not expecting anything."
"It says on the invoice they were ordered to your address by a Miss Andrea Walker."

"Oh if that's the case then ok."
"Where would you like the plants leaving?"
"Just around the back is fine."
"I tell you what love if you sign the delivery note now you can go back in. It's a bit chilly this morning."
Doreen watches from the kitchen window, as the delivery driver drops off plant after plant.
Andrea arrives home at a little after 4pm, as she walks around the back of the cottage a booming voice rings out a challenge.
"What do you think you are doing young lady?"
Andrea is startled and turns around.
"All those plants you bought."
"You looked upset when I couldn't talk this morning and I felt bad."
"Thanks so much sweetheart. You shouldn't have you need your money."
"I don't have a grandma anymore to spoil, so you are now officially my surrogate grandma."
Doreen smiles and feels warm and fuzzy inside.
"If I had to be adopted by a pretend Grandchild I would choose you every time Andrea."
"I have got some of that special compost again now. It's' a beautiful evening, so after tea I will do some planting and you can tell me all about some more of your adventures."
Three hours later all traces of Matthew have gone and the new plants look resplendent.

John wakes up the next morning having had a very strange and disturbing dream. In his dream he finds himself in a strange house with a women in a mask stood over him with a knife. He recalls at one point seeing the girls face without the mask but cannot recall her identity. It was one of those dreams where you wake up and instantly feel the relief of it not being real.

Two hours later John is driving to work and passes Big Worlds nursery, where he can see Andrea Walker in the playground and has an epiphany. The girl in his dream was Andrea of all people. He smirks to himself and thinks how did the girl of his dreams become the girl of his nightmares?" Ninety percent of adult males have thought the same thing since time in memorial.

John arrives at work and is still thinking about Andrea. More specifically about the bizarre dream he had about her. Richard was in a surprisingly good mood considering his present circumstances.
"Good morning mate."
"Morning, you seem to be in a good mood."
"Well has me and Rach are over, I have decided to move on."
"Which means what?"
"Which means I have met someone new on line and I stayed over last night!"
John thinks to himself. Leopards never really do change their spots do they?
"I had an encounter with a girl last night too."
"Get in mate."
"It's not what you think mate."

"Go on then."

"Can you remember that ID card we found belonging to Andrea Walker."

"I remember the ID but not the name."

"Well I took the ID back to her. We didn't speak but I saw her."

"So what about last night?"

"I dreamt she was wearing a mask and was trying to kill me."

"That's women for you mate. Crazy bitches the lot of them."

"It's in my head now. What could it mean?"

"I once saw a programme on dreams. They said your dreams are the opposite of what you think. So if you dream she is chasing you and hiding her face to kill you. It could mean you should be pursuing her for love not hate."

"That's an interesting theory dream Guru."

"It's probably bollocks but it's the only one I have got."

"She is lovely and I am sure she's not a killer."

"If you want her you need to make some moves pal."

John didn't yet know it, but this dream would be the start of an unhealthy obsession with Andrea. He had obsessed for many years about Emily and to this day he was still carrying a torch for her.

Andrea's lust for blood had been satisfied for now, but the next victim would still be in the back of her mind.

The police had recovered Matthews's car and had started yet another missing person enquiry. Matthew was the second man to disappear in just a few months. Enquiries into his personal life and finances gave no clues to the police. He was well liked and had a good support network of friends and family. He had no debts and there appeared to be no reason for him to disappear. The senior detective in the case had requested a full forensic examination of the car by CSI. Two sets of DNA had been recovered from the Honda. One Matthews and the other an unidentified female. It was Andreas, but having never come to the attention of the police, she was not on the data base.

"I think we need a day out somewhere Mags."
"If anyone needs a day out it's me. I am up to here with this place at the moment and all the whining parents." As she says" up to here" she raises her hand to her head.
"What about a day out in the smoke?"
"London."
"Why not it's only a couple of hours on the train. It will be a giggle."
"We can do some shopping have a meal and a few drinks and take in a museum."
"Good one Mags. I doubt you can even spell the word museum."
"Let's do it."
"How about Saturday?"
"Done."

Saturday arrives and Andrea and Mags meet at the station.

"I am ready for this."

"London won't know what's hit it."

The girls buy return tickets and thirty minutes later they are in the first class carriage courtesy of Andrea's generosity. They are having a Prosecco and watching the world go by.

Mags kicks off her heels and slouches down the seat so she can put her feet on the seat opposite.

"This is the life. I need to be rich I aren't meant to work."

"Me neither sister."

"This is going down well."

"Well you relax while I get another."

Andrea walks through to the bar in the next carriage. Already stood at the bar is a smartly dressed business man in his late 30's. Andrea looks down at the man's left hand, no sign of a wedding ring. She pretends to trip and nudges the man as she lunges forward.

"Sorry!"

"Its fine, are you ok?"

"Just a bit embarrassed."

"Don't worry there is nobody more clumsy than me."

They both laugh.

"Two more Prosecco's please."

"You are with company?"

"Girls day out."

"Business for me unfortunately."

"What's your business?"
"Believe it or not. I am a personal injury lawyer."
They both laugh again.
"I am pretty much sure I fell over a lose piece of carpet."
The man hands over a business card.
"If you ever need to talk about your injury give me a call. You know what give me a call even if you don't.
Andrea smiles at the man and gives a cheeky wink.
"Catch you later."
"Maybe."
Andrea goes from alluring to aloof in a matter of seconds. It's all part of the act.
"Guess what I have got?"
"Herpes."
"Cheeky bitch."
"No, I tripped and fell into this cute guy at the bar. We talked and he gave me his number."
"I don't know how you do it. Save some for me will you."
"You snooze you lose Mags."

John is at home bored and randomly Googling anything. He presses the return key and goes to make a cup of coffee. On his return he sees he has typed Andrea Walker. The only content on the page is the Big Worlds nursery website. He clicks on the website and presses the tab, marked staff. A picture of Andrea comes up and he saves it to his desktop. He spends the next few minutes drinking his coffee and staring at her picture. By mid-afternoon he had printed off her picture and stuck it to the wall above his bed. With one glance he had become totally besotted by her. She occupied his every waking hour since the dream. As a teenager he had worshipped Emily only for her to be taking from him. Maybe he should admire her from a far for a while to avoid a second broken heart. He goes back to the laptop and onto Facebook. There are 23 Andrea Walkers in the search results. Eventually after some furious clicking. He comes across her profile and selects the about feature. Born 25/08/78, Place of Birth, Nocton, Status, and Single. His next port of call is to look through her pictures. The most recent ones being taken that day in London. She appears to be with the women he had handed the ID and lanyard to.

Chapter 8
Obsession

Andrea was tired from her day in London with Mags. She runs a bath and adds some bubbles before jumping in and instructing the Amazon Echo in the hallway to play relaxing music. She wakes up 40 minutes later, with the water surrounding her freezing. She takes out the plug and quickly dives out, only to find there are no towels. She stoops low and makes her way into the spare bedroom trying not to show off her naked body to the world through the open blinds. Eventually she makes her way to the drawer containing fresh towels. She emerges onto the landing moments later wearing a large bath sheet and a towel turban. A towel turban is a total girl skill, men can't even contemplate.

She goes back into her room and plugs in the GHD's. Straitening her hair was a necessary evil, she hated. Stood up against a perfume bottle on the dressing table is the business card, the man on the train and given her Harvey Miles. Claims solicitor 07773 765675.

Andrea knows Harvey will not be the easy prey Matthew was. She was however confident her cunning and charms would prove to be more than a match for Mr Miles. It would take a few more days contemplation before she would consider calling.

Richard is sat in his kitchen drinking Jack Daniels. The uplifted mood and talk of a recent conquest was all lies. His life had fallen apart and he had tried to put on a front to hide his low mood. The Philandering and messing around was a coping mechanism. Five years ago he had left the army on a medical discharge. Having been diagnosed with PTSD after his best friend had been beheaded by the Taliban in Afghanistan. He had all the CBT and anti-depressants the army could muster without any success. The only way he could get through the days was to try be someone else. That someone else was now disappearing as the real Richard re-emerged. Richard had been drinking all night and was fighting the dark thoughts rushing through his mind. It was now 9.30am and John had been sent round to Richards because he hadn't turned up at work. At this point John thought his mate had probably stayed over at some random birds and forgotten to set the alarm. John went around the back of the house because Richard was one of those people who never really uses the front door.
The back door is slightly ajar and John shouts.
"Rich, Rich it's me."
He tried again only this time louder. There was still no answer so he opened the door and walked in.
Richard is slumped over the kitchen table unconscious. He is still holding an empty packet of Fluoxetine. The Jack Daniels bottle is empty. He reaches for Richards pulse at the neck. It is feint but he is still alive. He takes out his mobile and rings three nines.

"Emergency services which service do you require?"

"Ambulance please. There is an unconscious male, with a shallow pulse. Possible drink and drugs overdose."

Ten minutes later the ambulance arrives and Richard is rushed to A and E. John cannot believe this has happened to his friend. Only a few days ago he was back to being the larger than life character he always was. John was catapulted back in time to that dreadful day at Perthwaite. When he had been pulled out of the exam by the Principle, prior to learning of his mums demise. Everyone he cared for in this world seemed to either die or be taken away from him. Richard had been a good friend to John since he arrived at Brookes. He just hoped he would pull through.

For the next couple of days it was touch and go for Richard. His stomach had been pumped but he was showing early signs of some organ failure. Rachel and Bethany had come down from Scotland to see him. Whatever Rachel thought of Rich he was still Beth's father.

Back at work the days dragged by for John without his best friend. At home he had become quite a recluse. The solitude was beginning to play with his mind and his unhealthy obsession with Andrea was growing like an aggressive cancer within him.

Andrea is sat in the garden with her laptop checking out Mr Miles on Social media. The only result of her investigation was a Facebook account that appeared to be somewhat unused for the past 18 months. The pictures he did have were mainly pretentious stuff, like posing with an Aston Martin all be it an older DB9. Strange that she can identify an Aston Martin now but weeks ago was clueless about an Audi S3. Serial killers are of cause world class liars. Andrea was now even more determined to make Harvey her next victim. He was making fortunes on the back of people's misery. This was something she despised. With her contempt for Harvey growing she decides to go inside and make the call.

She makes her way up to her bedroom and picks the business card up from the dresser. Andrea lies back on her bed card in one hand mobile in the other. After a few minutes of deliberation she dials.
"Hello Harvey Miles, how can I help you?"
"Hi there Miles. I want to speak to you about an accident I have had."
Harvey can already smell a money making opportunity.
"What happened?"
"I tripped on a train and fell into a handsome stranger."
"Amanda?"
"Andrea actually! Amanda must be another girl. That said, we only met for a few minutes and it was over a week ago."
"I told you I was clumsy. In thought and deed or so it seems."

"I enjoyed our talk on the train and I have been curious about you ever since."

"I was hoping you would call. It's not every day beautiful girls fall into me."

"While I am in the mood for taking the initiative I would like to ask you out on a date."

"What would my mother say?"

"She's not coming is she?"

"Alas not, she died 18 months ago."

Even serial killers can feel empathy and Andrea felt bad.

"I am so sorry."

"Its fine you couldn't have known."

"I was thinking Picollinos in Nocton Saturday night, say 8pm. I take it you like Italian food."

"Sound delightful Andrea."

Andrea is now sat up on her bed with the phone on speaker. She is playing with the lock knife, opening and shutting the blade.

"Ouch!"

"What's up?"

"I am walking around with the phone and I just stubbed my toe."

"In that case I will reluctantly let you go."

"Looking forward to seeing you Saturday."

Andrea hadn't really stubbed her toe. She had accidentally run her finger across the open blade of the knife and cut her finger. Blood was now dropping onto her bedroom carpet. What irony, after her careful slaughter of Matthew.

John is in work and doing some stocktaking when Andrew the Dealer Principle walks in.

"John can you please come through into the training room?"

John follows Andrew in and sits with his colleagues. Andrew walks to the front of the room.

"I can honestly say this is one of the worst things I have ever had to do, in my 22 years in the motor trade. This morning I received the awful news that Richard passed away overnight. The suspected cause being acute organ failure. He was a much valued colleague and I know many of you were friends, especially you John. We will be having a collection to get some flowers and a sympathy card for his estranged wife Rachel. It's now mid-afternoon and I would ask the business and sales managers to clear today's appointments to get you all home to your loved ones. It seems the right thing to do on a day like today."

John can't believe his best friend was gone. He felt very, very alone in the world.

He grabs his coat and makes his way to the car park. Happy for the flyer but with no loved ones in his life the sentiment was a hollow one.

Andrea is putting away toys, wiping dirty faces and getting ready to leave Big Worlds for the day. Her next duty is to stand by the gate and hand the little darlings back to a line of parents, nans and childminders.

"Alfie, mummy's here."

The little boy pushes his way to Andrea and she hands him over to mum.

"Sophie, Sophie Taylor."
As Andrea turns to locate Sophie a boy runs straight passed her and into the road. There is a screech of brakes and time seems to stand still.
John's heart is in his mouth as the BMW comes to a rest, literally inches away from the boy.
He gets out still visibly shaken.
"Is he ok."
Andrea is now holding the little boy in her arms and is stroking his head.
She looks up at John and smiles. John is overjoyed to see Andrea but if anything a little star struck.
"He's fine, thanks to your lightning reflexes."
Struggling for words he says.
"Oh ok I will be off then."
John returns home and goes straight to his bedroom to stare at the goddess on his wall.
He knew where she worked now was the time to find out where she lived. Fifteen minutes later after a quick interrogation on some address finder sites he has the answer.
The Old Blacksmiths cottage
Dove Road,
Nocton.

The police enquiry into Matthews's disappearance had gone nowhere. Teams from the military, Mountain Rescue and the force helicopter had conducted searches over the last two weeks without success. Cell site analysis had brought back no hits on his phone. His passport was found at his home and there was no joy from Automatic number plate recognition (ANPR). The only clues being the car was seemingly abandoned at a pub and the unidentified female DNA.

John was restless it was now 2.30 am. His thoughts were not letting him sleep. It kept replaying events in his mind. His mum's death, losing Emily and now Richards's suicide. He jumps off the bed and puts on a black hoody and jeans. He makes his way quietly down the stairs and leaves via the front door closing it gently. He opens the car door and rolls off the sloped drive, before starting the engine. Ten minutes later he is on Dove Road, which is Andreas street. He parks the car a couple of hundred meters away and walks in the direction of her house. As he gets within a few metres of her garden he puts his hood up before climbing over the gate. He then edges his way down the sidewall of the cottage. There are no streetlights and the only illumination is provided by the moon. There are no lights on at the cottage or the surrounding houses. Andrea's rear garden has a long lawn with a stone path leading down to the old blacksmiths shop. John can see flashes of white going from side to side in the darkness. As he gets closer he can see Andrea has left some washing out. He pulls an item from the line and tucks it under his hoody. The silence is pierced by a dog barking and John climbs back over the gate and trots to his car. He drives home and parks his car a little way down the street.

A few moments later he is in his bedroom and now free to see what lout he had taken from Andreas.

He pulls out the item from inside his hoody. To his delight it's a lacy white thong. He was now party to Victoria's Secrets but luckily not Andreas. John forensically examines every thread of the thong before placing it on his bed post next to Andrea's photo. For a fleeting moment he feels ashamed of what he has done. The emotion passes over him and he falls asleep.

Five hours later John is awoken by the alarm. Had he just dreamt the events of the night before? He looks to his left and sees the lacy thong still hanging from his bed post. He smiles to himself.

Andrea was having a day off from Big Worlds and was contemplating her outfit for Saturday's reunion with Harvey. She decides to go classy sexy with a little black dress and heals. She even lines up the earrings and necklace she will wear on top of her jewellery box. The only deliberation was underwear. She imagined Harvey would appreciate some lacy briefs and would be a considerate lover in comparison to Matthew. Somewhere she has her favourite Victoria's Secret thong. It was not in her knicker draw or the washing basket which was empty. Then she has an epiphany and recalled doing the washing yesterday. She looks at the washing line from the bedroom window with no joy.

It's nearly midday and Andrea is in the garden taking the rest of her washing from the line and checking the garden for the missing knickers. A familiar voice comes from behind the fence.

"What's up love?"

"I can't find my knickers."

"Sounds like a good night."

"No not like that! They were on the line in the garden and now they are not."

"I haven't seen them over my side. It's not really been windy."

"I guess they have been stolen, bloody perverts!"

"I always know when mine are being stolen. It takes two guys to fold them and one to forklift them to the car."

"Oh Doreen you're so funny."

"Why don't you tell the police?"

"You know what? I am not 100% sure they have been taken and I don't want to waste their time."

In truth, the last thing Andrea wanted was the police sniffing around for her knickers. Andrea goes back into her cottage and contemplates the fate of her missing thong. Oh well she thought, maybe it's a commando job after all. Her next job was to exhume the blood from her bedroom carpet. Blood stains on the carpet was the kind of thing that might warn off even the most enthusiastic of potential lovers. The trouble with blood is even a spilled thimble full looks like a scene from a horror movie. Andrea's carpet cleaning is interrupted by a call from Mags.

"Hi love how are you doing? I missed you at work today."

"It's just been a relaxing day apart from the fact someone appears to have stolen a pair of my knickers."

"Clean or dirty."

"Clean not dirty like you."

"Moiré."

"Yer, you scruffy bitch."

Maggie had known Andrea far too long to be insulted by such a remark.

"It's probably the solicitor you met on the train. He seemed too good to be true."

"Jealousy will get you nowhere Mags."

"Where they expensive?"

"Victoria's Secrets."

"Waste of money babe. No man gives a shit if there Agent Provocateur or Primark when their ripping them off."

"You have such a way with words Mags."

"If you mean I tell the truth then yer. I guess I am just not a classy girl like you."

"Your amazing Mags. That's why you are my besty."

"I hope you are in work tomorrow, because I can't take cleaning up any more puke."

"Sounds like it's been an amazing day at Big Worlds."

"Four sent home with stomach bugs."

The friends carry on talking for another hour like only girls can.

Harvey in a bar with one of his colleagues.

"It's been a tough day mate. I need this drink."

"Tough days make money pal."

"Not on this occasion they don't. The business went to court on a slip and injury case and the judge threw it out."

"It happens."

"Seventy six year old with a broken pelvis. Should have been looking at 35% of 50k"

"Fuck it mate. Just move on to the next just like women."

"Talking of women. I have got a date on Saturday night with a hot blonde I met on the train."

"Lucky you, I will be staying in with Jackie, pretending I actually give a fuck about the X factor or Ant and Dec."

"Never mind mate I will take you out the weekend after this. Just remember to stay out of the sun to keep the tan line away from the wedding ring."

"You would never catch me cheating on Jackie."

"You didn't say you wouldn't do it, you just said you wouldn't get caught."

"Hopefully she would have my balls has earrings."

Chapter 9
Dashing from the date

John had just found out the date of Richard's funeral. Rich must have spoken about him to Rachel because he had been formerly invited to the funeral and the wake. Not only would he have to go through the trauma of his best mate's burial. He would have to spend a couple of hundred quid on a black suit and tie. One thing he had learned from his dad was to always show respect to the dead.

Saturday morning arrived and John had gone into town to buy a black suit. Also in town by chance was Andrea, who had dragged Mags along to buy replacement knickers. John tried shop after shop in his black suit quest. He was clearly reluctant to spend fortunes on something he would hopefully only wear once. The rule of thumb is, if you buy a black suit at 75 it gets way more use than if you are 35.

Andrea by contrast, had completed her purchase with consummate ease. She had merely gone back into the store and bought the exact same pair. Mags and Andrea were now free to leisurely enjoy their morning together.

"I bet you have got all your clothes for tonight all lined up and organised already."

"You know me too well."

"I am more of a throw whatever on at the last minute kind of girl."

"I need coffee to keep me awake tonight."

"Is that some of the night or all of the night?"

"We will have to see if he's a lucky boy or not."

Andrea and Mags make their way to Costa, where they order ham and cheese Paninis' and two vanilla lattes. They take their regular seat in the corner near the window. A few minutes later John too goes into Costa and orders a cappuccino. He sits opposite the far wall only maybe 15 to 20 feet away from the girls. As he looks up he immediately notices its Andrea. Had he passed her in the street, he would have probably said hello. However he didn't feel comfortable going across to their table to say hello. Though he desperately wanted to. Andrea and Mags were so busy talking they wouldn't have noticed him if he was Tom Cruise.

"Show us your knickers them Andrea."

"What in here?"

"I aren't asking you to wave them around like a bloody flag. I was thinking I might get some has my lucky pants."

"Mine got stolen they are hardly bloody lucky."

Andrea reluctantly takes out the thong partially shielded by the bag. From where John is sat he can see one of a matching pair. The other one was still hanging from his bed post. He takes out his mobile phone and props it up on the table like he is reading something. He selects the camera mode then 2.5 times zoom. As Andrea faces Mags he takes a picture. He does this multiple times in a matter of seconds. Thirty five images in total. The girls take about 20 minutes to eat their lunch and leave. Once they have gone John quickly flicks through the images. That evening he prints of all 35 images and sticks them to the wall in the order they were taken. The images were taken so close together you could put them in a book and flick through them to cause a simple animation. Like you would by drawing a stick man kicking a football multiple times with slight changes. John had taken a second souvenir from his trip to Costa. Andrea had wiped her mouth on a serviette which was lipstick stained. John had picked it up on the way out apparently unconcerned if he had been seen or not. He is sat on the bed holding it to his face. It has a slight accent of her perfume.

Andrea was getting ready for her date with Mr Miles AKA Harvey. The little black dress had been superseded by a deep red off the shoulder number with a satin finish. In the true tradition of all women, the shoes and bag were also replaced to match the dress. Andrea clips on her earrings and sprays her neck and wrists with the nights preferred perfume Dior J'adore. She had no plans to do the deed, but should the opportunity present itself she wanted to be prepared. Andrea didn't like to leave anything to chance. The bed had been made with the water proof mattress liners under the sheets. The lock knife was under the pillow and the furnace was ready to light.

The doorbell rings and Andreas Uber had arrived.

She sits in the back of the C class Mercedes.

"Picolino's restaurant please on Cooper Street."

"A date is it?"

"Yes the first and maybe the only, you never know"

"Well I hope it goes well anyway."

Ten minutes later the Mercedes pulls up outside the restaurant.

Harvey is stood by the door waiting for her. He is wearing a deep pink blazer, white shirt and faded Levi jeans. He hoped the chemistry would be on point like the colour coordination.

"Good evening Andrea you look stunning."

"Why Mr Miles, you don't look half bad yourself."

Ever the gentlemen, Harvey holds the door open for Andrea. Their booking is checked and they are shown to a table in a quiet corner of the restaurant. It is a lovely spot for a romantic meal or a serial killers grooming. A few moments later a waiter comes over with the food and drinks menu.

"I haven't eaten all day."

"It's going to cost me then!"

"Why are you paying?"

"I asked you out so it's my treat. I am a modern women."

"I can't let you do that. Let's at least go Dutch."

"I struggle with the accent and clogs wouldn't really look right with this dress.

They both laugh.

"No I insist, you can pay next time."

"That sounds promising."

"Oh I am full of promise."

Andrea clearly likes Harvey, but she is a professional and will not let sentiment get in the way of her end game.

The couple order and a waiter appears with a bottle of wine.

"Would sir like to taste the wine?"

Andrea coughs. "No but Madam would."

The waiter pours a small amount of wine in to Andrea's glass. In the most pretentious way possible she swirls the wine in the glass then sniffs it. She takes a sip and nods.

"Lovely body."

"The waiter walks off.

"Yes lovely body. The wine tasted pretty good too."

"Keep talking like that and you might just get to find out."

"So what do you like to do Andrea?"

"You won't believe how exciting my life is. One of the highlights of my life at present is doing Doreen's garden next door."

"What do you do, just clip some plants and mow the lawn?"

"No, digging and planting."

"That's hard work."

"It certainly is, a real killer."

Inside Andrea is smiling to herself.

Andrea and Harvey spend the next three hours in each other's company. Harvey feels like there is some real chemistry. For Andrea it was a mix of genuinely liking Harvey, but with her eyes firmly fixed on the prize. Andrea decides to ramp up her desirability ratings by slipping off her shoe and gently stroking the inside of Harvey's thigh with her foot. On each stroke she gets nearer to his groin. Gushing with expectation, Harvey suggests they leave.

"Well I think it's about time to get going."

"Why the rush?" Andrea winks at Harvey.

"Bill please."

Five minutes later the bill is paid and Harvey and Andrea are stood outside the restaurant.

"What now then Andrea, have I been a good enough boy?"

Andrea pulls Harvey towards her and slips her tongue into his mouth. They kiss passionately.

"Oh no."

"What?"

"I think I might have forgotten to pick up my credit card."

"I will run in and get it for you." Harvey is anxious to speed up proceedings

Harvey goes back into the restaurant. Shortly after, the Uber Mercedes turns up to drop Andrea off. She climbs in, just as Harvey is coming back out onto the street. She looks over and blows a kiss at him as the car pulls away. Andrea enjoyed the thought of playing with her prey like a cat with a mouse.

The morning came and John was laid in bed holding the lipstick stained serviette to his face. He could still smell a slight aroma of Andrea's perfume. He knew that over the next few days the fragrance would die. He began to feel sad and a single tear feel from his eye onto it. As an idea pops into his head he begins to smile. If he can identify the perfume, he can buy some and replenish the smell on the serviette or even spray some elsewhere.

Two hours later John is making his way into Boots to visit the fragrance counters. He stands around a while trying to concoct a viable story about the serviette that might not seem too weird. He approaches the member of staff he envisages to be the most helpful.

"Excuse me can you help?"

"Certainly sir."

"This might sound a bit strange but I had a date the other day with a new girl. I wanted to buy her a present for when I see her next. She left her serviette behind and it smells of her perfume which was amazing."

John pulls the serviette from his pocket. In his mind, he already thought his story was a bit weird or was he just being paranoid.

"Let's have a smell love?"

John looks uncomfortable.

"I get asked stuff like this all the time. Mostly from clueless husbands."

The sales assistant has a couple of sniffs and pauses. She the walks away and returns with a bottle of perfume which she sprays on a card.

"There you go take a sniff."

"That's it."

"Christian Dior 'J'adore'"

"I will take a bottle please."

"That's £65 for 50ml or £94 for 100ml."

"I will take a 100ml please."

"Somebody is a lucky lady! Buying a near hundred pound bottle of perfume after one date."

"I just hope she is worth it."

"Well if she's not you can take me out you're a keeper."

The sales assistant was far from unattractive but clearly nearer 50 than 30.

"I might just do that."

Johns gets back to his car and speedily rips off the perfume packaging before applying some to his hand and seat head restraint.

Andrea is having a quiet morning and thinking about Harvey when the message alert goes on her phone.

"Now you see her now you don't!"

She replies.

"Everything good is worth waiting for."

"Well I thought?"

"You thought when we left the restaurant I would just drop my knickers and fall on my back?"

"Not quite like that, I at least thought that after we shared that kiss there would be more to come. "

Andrea ponders over her next answer.

"I am going to play a little game with you."

"Sounds interesting, I like games."

"I live where someone used to get shoes. The shoes are no good for them, you or me. The street where the bird of peace should be. You have one hour to take! Your prize."

Andrea made her usual pre-murder checks before slipping into some sexy underwear and a short silk dressing gown.

Fifty two minutes later the front doorbell rings. Andrea puts her head around the door then pulls Harvey in by the collar.

"Somebody is a very clever boy."

Andrea slips off the dressing gown and leads Harvey upstairs. She starts to kiss him as they go into the bedroom. She pushes him gently onto the bed and he sits. Andrea kneels on the floor in front of him and undoes his belt before gently pulling down his jeans and Calvin Klein's. She licks her lips like the most erotic of porn stars before taking his cock in her mouth. As she moves her mouth up and down the shaft of his penis he starts to groan. She takes him close to the point of climaxing and stops. By now, he will do anything Andrea wants. She takes off his shirt and lies him on the bed. She takes off her bra and slips her pants off, before opening the bed side cabinet draw. After a few seconds of rummaging she sits on Harvey and ties him to the bed with two pieces of silk ribbon before using a third to blindfold him. She grinds herself up and down Harvey and he is close to ejaculating. As the wave of climax comes over Andrea, she reaches for the lock knife and runs it across Harvey's cerotic artery the blood begins to spurt so she throws a pillow over his head. His feet begin to twitch and then fall silent. For all Andrea was a cold hearted killer this was her first venture into the world of picquerism.

Picquerism- is a sexual interest in penetrating the skin of another with sharp objects.

The deed was done. Andrea wrapped up the body has per her Modus Operandi. Harvey however would have to stay in situ until she could dispose of his body in the stealth of night. Her work done she settles down to watch TV and drink coffee, like nothing has happened. Suddenly a thought comes into her head. How did Harvey arrive at her house? It wouldn't do for his car to be found so close to her home. She rifles through the pockets of his jeans which are still on the floor. There is a key for a Range Rover Sport. She puts on a black hoody and a baseball cap and goes down to the bottom of the garden where she keeps a can of petrol for the mower. She decants some of the petrol into a glass bottle and shoves a rag down the bottle neck. She then carefully slips the Molotov cocktail into a carrier bag. Around 50 metres down the street from her house she comes across a gun metal grey Range Rover. She presses the open function on the key and the lights flash signalling the doors are open. She climbs into the driver's seat and reaches for the seat adjustment. Harvey was 6'1" Andrea is more 5' 2". She drives the Range Rover through some winding back roads and comes across an old dilapidated cattle shed. She reverses the Range Rover into the building, over some fractured asbestos cladding. Andrea takes off her hoody and baseball cap and throws them onto the driver's seat. She is now dressed in a sports top, leggings and trainers. She lights the rag and throws the bottle onto the rear seats. Within seconds the interior of the car starts to burn. As she exits the building the petrol tank explodes. She calmly runs off down the road, just like any other jogger getting in the hard miles.

By the morning Harvey had gone the way of Andrea's previous victims and was ready to be mixed with compost. The Range Rover keys had been thrown into the canal on her way home.

Five days later the police are opening up yet another missing person's case. Harvey hadn't turned up for work and the burnt out husk of his Range Rover had been found in a building off the B122. The Detective Chief Inspector leading all three missing people's enquiries couldn't help feel there was a serial killer on the loose. Though no bodies had been found, it was difficult to believe that three males with no issues financial or emotional should just disappear. The burnt out Range Rover confirmed in her mind that something sinister was afoot. A young Trainee Detective Constable enters the enquiry room.

"Ma'am, we have a picture of Harvey Miles car taken from an ANPR camera on Dawson Avenue."

The DCI looks over the shoulder of the young detective. The image is slightly blurry. It appears to show what looks like a youth wearing a dark hoody with the hood up and a baseball cap low over their face.

"Good job Adam, but it's no good for ID. It gives us a bit of a clue where the car might have come from. Get back on the ANPR stuff. We might have to consider private CCTV, Dash and bus cams."

John was completely oblivious to the extra-curricular activities of his love interest. He had been down to Costa that day. Where he had taken some images of himself sat in the seats Andrea and Mags liked to occupy. Thanks to having the photos he had taken of the girls on his phone at the location. He was able to sit in the position Mags was in when Andrea showed her the knickers.

On his return home he is sat at his computer on photo shop. He is trying to replace Mags image with his own. So it looks like Andrea is showing him the knickers she had bought and they look like a couple. After a frustrating evening he is finally happy with the result. He prints one off for the wall and a smaller one on photo paper to slide into his wallet. To be in relationship was all he wanted. Since Richard's death he felt so isolated and alone and was spiralling further and further into an unhealthy fantasy world.

Mags and Andrea are at work.

"I forgot to ask you how that date went with the guy on the train."

"Well it went well to some extent."

"What do you mean?"

"Well it was a nice meal and he was good company, but I couldn't help but feel he was a bit of a pretentious wanker."

Andrea looks around conscious of the fact she had just said "Wanker" with small children around.

What would she do if a child asked her what it meant?

As she imagines the following scenarios she smiles.

Little girl. "Miss what's a wanker?"

"You will know when you're married."

Little boy. "Miss what's a wanker?"

"When you grow up you will be one."

She would love to explain her hypothesis to Mags, but to do so would mean saying it again.

"What do you mean? "

"He was just full of himself. Talking about how much money he makes and stuff."

"Anything else?"

"Oh yer, he was a shit kisser too. His snogging was that bad, I pretended I had lost my bank card. He went back into the restaurant to get it for me.

When he came out I blew him a kiss as I went off in the taxi."

"I like your style."

"What are you doing tonight mags?"

"Not a great deal, Cora, wine and bed!"

"What about going out for a few drinks. We could go to that new pub near mine, with the new beer garden."

"Sounds good, have a chinwag and watch the world go by. "

"What about going straight after work. Its red hot today and I could do with the hydration."

"What about the cars"

"Leave your car here, we can walk from mine and put you in a taxi later. I can pick you up in the morning."

"Sorted."

John was looking at his Andrea gallery when the doorbell rang. It was an Amazon delivery.

He rushes downstairs and picks up the parcel before eagerly taking it upstairs to unwrap.

It was his new toy a Cannon camera complete with detachable zoom lens. When he first considered buying a camera many months ago, it was purely to take up photography. It was now just a tool to facilitate his Andrea obsession. After catching up with a few tutorials on YouTube and very vaguely look at the instructions he decides to venture out. His intention was to go out into the country and capture some images of birds and the occasional military planes that flew over.

Over at Big World, Andrea and Mags have just said goodbye to the final child and have their minds firmly set on a few ice cold G and Ts.

"Well that's it, jeez it's hot out here."

The girls get into the car and Andrea reaches into the glove compartment to find her shades.

After a couple of minutes of refreshing lipstick and putting on the blue lensed aviators she pulls off.

Ten minutes later they pull onto Andrea's drive.

"Right let's get some drinking done. "

"Is it far?"

"Just around the corner and a couple of 100 metres."

Mags pretends to crawl along the floor like a legionnaire who had been in the desert without water for days.

"Water, water, gin.gin."

"You bloody idiot."

Mags stands back upright and wipes a drop of sweat from her forehead before it drips into her eyes.

"I wonder if there will be any fit men there to look at."

"Well we are the girl eye candy. So I shouldn't see why there shouldn't be boy candy."

As they get closer to the pub they can see its dead.

"Typical nobody here."

"We are here and that's all that matters. It's 5pm not everybody yearns for alcohol like us."

"Hendricks ok for you babe?"

The girls walk into the pub and emerge a few minutes later carrying gin glasses you could keep a goldfish in. The drinks are adorned with summer fruits, cucumber and mini straws.

Mags and Andrea pick a spot directly in sunlight and take a sip of their gin through the mini straws.

"This is the life, sunshine on your face, gin and great company."

"So Mags what about you and fellas?"

"Well, strap yourself in. I had a few boyfriends in my late teen and early twenty's but nothing too serious. I worked in an office in 2002 and met this guy. He was wonderful and charming. You could say he swept me off my feet. We were together nearly 5 years. I came home early one day to find him and the girl from accounts enjoying a bedroom meal."

Andrea pauses for a moment to process what Mags had just told her.

"My God! You caught them doing a 69."

"Yep!"

"What did you do?"

"I just ran out. What could I say? Would you like onions and ketchup with that love?"

Andrea always admired Mags ability to make a joke of anything. She did however realise her friend must have been horrified and heart broken.

"Gosh that must have been hard to swallow."

Andrea's euphemism was meant to judge Mags feelings. If she laughed or replied with a witty retort she was ok.

Chapter 10
Maggie pulls

"I didn't stay long enough to see if she did or not."

Andrea places her hand on Mags arm.

"We need to find you a nice man who won't shit on you."

As she says those words to men take their seats and the table opposite. They are both in their late 30's and are more than just acceptable in the looks department. Andrea gently kicks Mags in the shin and nods her head in the direction of the men.

"There you go."

"They are nice, but for all my talk I am not super confident when it comes to guys."

"Leave it to me."

Andrea turns her head to the men.

"Hi guys do you mind giving us some company over here."

The two guys hastily pick up their drinks and join the girls.

"Hi I am Andrea and this is Maggie."

"I am Rob and this is Sam."

"Pleased to meet you both."

The group talk together for a while before Rob turns his attentions to speaking to Maggie.

"So Maggie is there a husband at home or a boyfriend."

"You get straight to the point don't you?"

Maggie starts to blush.

"Well if you don't ask."

"What about you are you in a relationship?"

"No free has a bird. I have never found the right one and that's why I am still looking."

"You have to kiss a lot of frogs before you find a prince or princess."

Rob does his best frog impression and they both laugh.

Andrea is talking to Sam.

"So Sam what's the story with you?"

"I was married for ten years until my wife died of breast cancer last year. I have twins both aged 5."

"I am so sorry."

"The twins ask me all the time, where mummy is."

Andrea had no interest in taking a single dad away from his young children. For all her evil she had always picked victims without a significant other or children.

John has driven into the country and walked up a public foot path to a hill probably 500/600 feet above sea level.

He has been trying to focus in on a falcon trying to hunt something down in the valley below. Most of his shots were terribly out of focus. The beauty of photography in the digital ere meant he could just press delete. He can now see a couple away in the distance starting to ascend the hill. He focuses in and captures a detailed shot of the women. Capturing images of women was his forte after all. Happy with his work he decides to stay a little longer. He deletes the picture of the women who must have been all of 60 and not particularly attractive.

Two hours later Andrea has left her friend talking to Rob. Sam feeling very gooseberry like had also left leaving Mags and Rob to their privacy.

"I can't believe they have both just gone."

"Oh well it gives us a chance to get to know each other a little."

In truth Andrea had been a perfect wing women, calling the guys over then bugging out at the ideal time.

"Right Maggie I really need to go. Would you mind if I had your phone number. Maybe we can do this again without matchmakers."

"If you pass me your phone I will tap it in."

"Only if you promise you won't run off with it."

"There you go. Ring me now and I will have your number."

Rob leans forward and gives Maggie a continental air kiss on each cheek. He pauses for a second before kissing her gently on the lips. He then walks off.

A few hours later Maggie is at home about to go to bed and thinking about Rob.

She sends him a text.

"By the way I loved your little kiss earlier."

She stays awake a little longer, awaiting in a reply. Her wait is in vain and she goes to bed. She falls asleep quickly aided by the effects of the gin. The morning comes and she is trying to bring herself round after a peaceful night's sleep. She is startled by the bleeping of her text alert. Anxious to see if it's Rob she dives out of bed and stubs her toe.

"Bastard!"

The pain eventually passes over her and she pick up her phone. There is a text notification from Rob.

"I loved the kiss too. I hoped you didn't mind."

Like an excited 15 year old teenager she replies.

"I can't wait for some more. XXX."

"Do you fancy going out for a meal on Thursday night my treat. Whatever you like Italian. Indian. Mexican, Chinese. "

Maggie hadn't been on a proper date for such a long time. She is very nervous but excited.

"I would love to X."

Maggie cannot wait to get to work and tell Andrea. The doorbell rings, it is Andrea. In the excitement of the night before she had completely forgotten that she had left her car at work and was being given a lift to work.

"Morning Mags, got any gossip for me?"

"Well yes, I exchanged numbers with Rob. He kissed me last night ant text me this morning. "

"When you say kiss do you mean tongue down the throat stuff."

"No just a gentle peck on the lips."

"It's a start Mags. Maybe we need another visit to Victoria's Secrets for some lucky pants."

"Oh I forgot, your theory was what? No man is worried about the label in the back when he's ripping them off."
"He's taking me out on a date on Wednesday night."

"Where to?"

"A restaurant of my choice."

"So will you be giving him a treat after his meal?"

"A lady never tells."

"Yes, but what about you."

"What do you want a blow by blow account."

"So there might be blowing."

"As if I would do such a thing on a first date. Well maybe the second."

"You will be fine love, whatever happens, happens."

"All this smutty talk is making me late for work."

"We don't have to set off for another 15 minutes."

"Do me a favour Andrea, make me a coffee. I am dehydrated from last night."

"The gin or the kissing?"

"I don't know they were both delicious."

"What about Sam."

"Lovely guy but not for me. Five year old twins and still mourning his dead wife."

John was on his way to work and the inside of his car had a distinctive smell of J'adore. Today was the day he would get a new partner in crime to replace Richard. As he gets into work Andrew is stood with the new guy.

"Morning John, This is your new colleague Martin.

"Morning mate pleased to meet you."

"If you want to go through to the parts department with John he will show you the ropes."

Martin was in his early 30's and slightly chubby wearing round rimmed glasses. He spoke with a North East accent. Luckily not so strong that John couldn't understand.

"The boss told me about what happened to the last guy. He said you were quite close."

"Yes, he was a great mate."

The conversation is interrupted by one of the technicians coming into the department.

"We are ordering sandwiches for breakfast if you are interested John?"

"I would love a bacon and egg please."

"Do you want anything mate?"

"I will have the same please mate."

"How much are they?"

The technician checks the menu.

"Two pounds fifty mate."

"I just need to pop out to the car to get some money."

"No worries mate I will get yours."

John reaches into his wallet and pulls out a fiver. AS he does so the picture of Andrea falls out of his wallet to the floor near Martins feet.

The technician walks out and John hastily picks up the photo. Martin averts his eyes like he hasn't seen it.

"So obviously not from round here judging by the accent."

"I met a local girl at university and now we are married."

"What about you John do you have a partner?"

"No I am strictly single."

Martin had seen the picture on the floor and was a little puzzled by Johns answer, though he didn't question it.

Martins first day at Brookes passed by with no more dramas and John felt happy to have someone to talk to.

On John's return home, he went straight up to his bedroom to say hello to his collection of Andrea images. The wall was still looking pretty blank and he felt the need to fill it. He decided he would go out later and test out his new founded skills.

Andrea is at home changing into some old jeans and a T-shirt. She was going round to Doreen's to do some more planting using her special compost. Harvey had been hanging around in the shed at the bottom of the garden for far too long. Andrea always felt relieved to get the evidence off the premises, even if it was only next door. It's another glorious summer evening and Doreen was already sat in the garden with some cold lemonade and a book. Andrea makes her way down to the bottom of the garden and reappears moments later with her Harvey Miles vintage compost. A smile comes across her face as she wonders which brand of victim compost grows the best flowers. It was literally a case of which man was the more fertile. She is still smiling as enters Doreen's garden.

"Good evening Doreen. Here I am has promised to sort out your hydrangeas."

"You carry on love and I will get you a nice cold lemonade."

"Thanks Doreen. It's going to be warm work." As she says this she wipes a bead of sweat from her brow. Andrea drags the hydrangeas to the bottom of the garden and begins her task. She digs the first hole and reaches into the bag for a handful of compost. Andrea can feel something smooth and hard in the bag. Surely this can't be a piece of bone because they have always turned to ash overnight. She shakes the compost from round the object and looks at her hand. The misshaped piece of gold was probably a signet ring. Doreen appears with the lemonade.

"There you go love, get that down you."

"Thankyou."

Andrea quickly stuffs the piece of gold into her pocket. She was kicking herself for making such a stupid mistake and not noticing the ring on Harvey's hand.

"I know what I meant to ask you Andrea. A couple of weeks ago, I had my window open in the bedroom because it was so hot and I could smell smoke. Did you smell it?"

"I certainly did Doreen. Don't worry it was only me, I was burning some old rubbish in the old furnace in the blacksmiths workshop."

"You still use it."

"It's a win win. No trips to the dump site for me and I get to think about how my great grandad would have felt when it was a working blacksmiths shop."

"I remember your dad doing much the same thing."

John's car is parked on the road behind Andrea's garden. He is snapping away at his chosen subject. He can see her gardening, but she cannot see him. He pauses as a couple of cars drive past. When they pass he starts to view the images, which are like a story book. The first images are of Andrea through her open bedroom window then walking to the bottom of the garden and into Doreen's. Happy with the results of his latest reconnaissance mission he returns home.

The next morning Martin is walking down the road with his three year old daughter Abby. They are making their way to Big World for her first day at nursery.

"Daddy do I have to go, can I just stay with mummy?"

"No darling mummy is at work today."

Abby squeezes her daddies hand and gives him a big appealing wide eyed look. Martin was very protective of his daughter and in truth felt just has apprehensive.

They enter the building and are met by a strawberry blonde haired women in her early 30s.

"Good morning, this is my daughter Abby Wright. She is here for her first day."

"Good morning Mr Wright. I am Andrea one of the nursery nurses here at Big World."

"I think she's a little nervous."

"It's only natural."

Andrea takes hold of Abby's hand. "Come on sweetheart let's go and find some toys."

Martin bends down and kisses Abby before walking off.

For some reason, he cannot put his finger on he recognises Andrea. But where from? He is still racking his brain when he arrives at Brookes.

"Good morning mate."

"Good morning John."

Suddenly it hits him. The girl at the nursey was the girl in the picture John had dropped from his wallet. He was busting to ask John, but thought better of it.

Abby's first day at Big World went well, once she was engrossed with new friends and toys. Her mum had picked her up and Andrea reported the good news back to her.

"Well Mags, it's the big night tonight. "

Andrea gets up close to Maggie to smell her breath.

"Breath needs to be a bit more minty love."

"Cheeky bitch."

"Well if you want some more kisses lady."

"It's all in hand. I have taken a leaf out of your book. The outfits hung up and my new Vicky's Secrets lucky pants are still in the carrier bag."

"What about protection?"

"I have got a Taser in my handbag. If all else fails I'll cut his throat with my lock knife."

Wow thought Andrea! That remark was just a little too close to home.

"You know what I mean."

"All good love still got the coil."

"Never fancied that, it all seems a bit industrial."

"What, you a Jack and Jill girl are you?"

"If you mean by your very poor attempt at a casting for EastEnders, pill then yes"

"I find it all too easy to forget in the morning. The last thing I want is getting knocked up on a one night stand in my 40s."

"One night stand is it?"

"You know what I mean. One night, two night, god knows. What will be will be?"

"You will knock him dead Mags your gorgeous."

"I don't think, I knock em dead like you do babe."

Andrea smiles to herself at yet another bang on the money comment.

"Do you know where you are going yet?"

"No he's picking me up at 7.30."

"I am sure he will treat you right."

"Because he wants to get into my pants."

"No, because he seemed nice you silly mare."

Three hours later Mags is on pins. She is looking forward to the night and seeing Rob, but hasn't been on a date for a year or so. Finding her ex in bed with another women had done very little for her confidence. The clock ticks by to 7.25pm. Mags is dressed in a white top and faux leather mini skirt. Had she put her picture on a dating site for the over 40s, she would no doubt be inundated with potential suitors. The doorbell rings and Mags answers. Rob is stood at the door with a long stemmed single red rose. He hands over the flowers to Mags and kisses her on the cheek.

"Your carriage awaits, beautiful."

Mags blushes and opens the front passenger door of Robs Volvo.

"Do you like Chinese food Maggie?"

"Love it and please call me Mags, it's what I am used to."

John is at home sticking the 247 pictures he had taken of Andrea to his bedroom walls. He was debating whether to put the best head shots near his bed and close to him, or on the opposing wall so he could see them as he woke up. He still hopes that one day he would gather the personal bravery to ask her out. Until then he would just have to enjoy collecting Andrea related objects for his shrine.

Andrea has received yet another Facebook message from an admirer.

"Hi I have seen your profile and think you are really cute. I know from your about info that you are still single" Andrea was contemplating replying when her phone rings.

"Hi love it's me."

"What's up Mags?"

"I don't know, I guess I just feel a bit apprehensive about this date with Rob. What if he wants to sleep with me, what should I do?"

Andrea can hardly believe that 40-year-old women was asking her such a question.

Chapter 11
An uneasy feeling

"Mags, what can I say. All you can do is do what you feel is right. That said don't be pressurised into it."
"Should I tell him what happened?"

"Hell no, that would be so weird. If you want him to run to the hills then go ahead."

"I need to go anyway, I am in the loo."

"You will be fine Mags. You know I am always here for you."

Andrea returns to the Facebook message and deletes it. Mags for all her frailties, had inadvertently saved a man's life. Andrea couldn't help but think about her friend for the rest of the night.

Back in the restaurant mags has just returned to the table.

"Are you ok?"

"This Prosecco is going straight through me. That said you can pour me another glass."

Rob pours half a glass into Mags glass.

"I don't want you thinking I am trying to get you drunk."

"Who said you had to try get me drunk."

They both laugh and Rob leans forward to kiss Mags on the lips.

Maggie doesn't know if it's the company or the Prosecco, that's making her feel so relaxed. She clearly feels an attraction for Rob she had not felt for a man in many years.

Two hours later the meal is over and Rob and Mags are outside.

"I will drop you off at home if that's ok Mags?"

"That's ok if you drop yourself off at my house too."

Mags had decided to take Andreas advice and go with the flow. She was an adult and if she wanted to sleep with Rob, she shouldn't feel guilty.

Ten minutes later they arrive at Maggie's house. They both feel slightly awkward as they walk into the front room.

"Well what now?"

They share a deeply passionate kiss and fall onto the sofa.

"Well at least that cut out all the, are you coming in for coffee cliché shit."

The couple carry on kissing and rob is feeling Maggie's breasts over her top.

"Let me help you."

Maggie undoes the top three buttons of her top and Rob slips his hand in to unhook her bra. She shivers with delight as he caresses her nipples. He then moves his hand to her knee and up the outside of her thigh. For a split second she freezes as her ex's infidelity comes to mind. The thought passes and she reaches her hand over to pull away at Robs zip.

They both stop when they realise the curtains are still open.

"Let's carry on where we left off upstairs."

Andrea is feeling reassured that her friend hadn't called her again. She opens up the bedroom windows to let some air in. It is another stifling night. Feeling warm and tired she falls asleep on the bed naked.

Two hours later John is dressed in all black and making his way down the side of Andreas house. It is a darker night than on his last visit with no moonlight. As he edges his way down the garden wall he comes across Andreas wheelie bin. He gently opens the lids and uses the torch on his mobile to illuminate the inside. He quietly searches through the bin. There are no signs of trophies, just rotting food and packaging.

John continues his way to the back of the house safe in the knowledge that Andreas neighbour is an old lady and not an elite soldier or police officer. At the back of the house is an orangery and just above that, Andreas bedroom. John uses the drain pipe to make his way onto the orangery roof. Being careful not to slip onto the glass below. He eases himself up on the window ledge and can see Andrea laid out naked on the bed asleep. He watches her for few minutes before deciding she was sound asleep enough to take a photo. As he eases the mobile phone from his pocket his foot slips from under him and he puts his hand on the window to steady himself. He takes his photo and is about to go when he notices a hair brush on a chair near the window. He eases himself over the window ledge onto his stomach and reaches for the brush. He is at the extremes of his reach but manages to grab the brush. Andrea moves and turns onto her back. John slides down the side of the orangery and twists his knee. It hurts but he has no time to attend to his injury. He quickly scrambles his way around the side of the house and runs off.

John had the holy grail of all stalkers he had managed to see his victim naked. On his return home he prints off a picture of her and adds it to his collection. As he takes off his black hoody, the hair brush falls to the floor. He had completely forgotten about the brush. John sits on a chair and painstakingly pulls out every hair. With his task complete he ties it together with some cotton and sprays it with J'adore. He then puts it in an envelope and slips it under his pillow.

By the morning the wind is blowing a little stronger and the curtains are blowing into the room. Andrea leaps out of bed to shut the window. As she pulls the window to, she can see a palm print on the outside of the glass. Still half asleep she quickly dismisses the palm print and walks to the bathroom to shower. Ten minutes later she walks back into the bedroom having washed her hair. She takes the towel from her head and starts to look for her brush. After a few minutes of looking in all the most obvious places she begins to feel frustrated. Andrea is pretty sure she had left it on the chair by the open window. The window with the unexplained palm print. She begins to feel very uneasy because the last thing she wanted to do was to get the police involved. Considering her options she carries on with her morning routine before work.

John wakes up and opens one eye. He focuses on the pictures around his room eventually settling his vision on the recently acquired naked picture of

Andrea. He is aroused because his last sleep was REM and the testosterone levels increase. It is a common misconception it was because of the subject of a dream.

Chapter 12
Experience is everything

Feeling further aroused because of Andreas picture he starts to masturbate. A few moments later he finishes himself off and goes into the bathroom to clean up.

Andrea arrives at work early, not because she is particularly conscientious, but because she is keen to catch up on the sordid details pf Maggie's date.

"Morning Mags, you look like the cat that got the cream."

"Oh great let's start the day with a massive euphemism."

The irony being this sentence was also a massive euphemism.

"Well Mags did you enjoy the night?"

"Yes Andrea I can say I really enjoyed the night."

"Did you?"

"If I tell you I really enjoyed some of the morning too."

"So you did the deed. Maggie is back on the bike."

"You make it sound so sordid."

"I was worried after you ring me last night."

"I did like you said and went with the flow. There was a moment when things were heating up and I froze for a second. I was thinking about my ex and what happened."

"I get that completely but Rob isn't your ex is he."

"He is a lovely guy. He is coming over on Saturday and staying over."

"I am so pleased for you Mags, you deserve happiness."

"I just hope this is the start of something good."

Andrea is thinking about the handprint and is wanting to get Mags perspective on things.

"Mags I don't know if I am being paranoid or losing my mind?"

"I woke up this morning with the wind blowing the curtains through the open window. When I went to shut the window there was a hand print on the glass and I can't find my hair brush."

"Wow that's a bit disturbing. Are you sure your brush is missing. I left it on a chair near the window."

"If you are sure you need to go to the police."

"That's the problem Mags I aren't completely sure and I don't want to waste police time."

"What about getting some cameras or even a dog."

"The cameras might be a good idea but I don't have the time for a dog. I wouldn't want to leave it all day while I am at work it's unfair."

"The least you can do is make sure your windows and doors are locked."
"I don't care how hot it is in the bedroom the windows are staying shut."
"You could always stay at mine a few nights if you are scared."
"Thanks Mags but Ménage trois, isn't really my thing." The girls laugh

After some soul-searching Andrea decides to have covert cameras installed covering the rear garden and the side of the cottage.

John's obsession with Andrea was growing by the day and he had continued to masturbate almost daily as he fantasied over her picture. In truth John was still a virgin and had experienced no sexual acts with any women. He longed to make love to Andrea and the thought occupied his every waking hour. John had no confidence with women and the last thing he wanted, was to mess it up if he ever had the balls to ask Andrea out. He had briefly toyed with going on Tinder or one of the no strings meet up and fuck sites. Having thought about it over the past few weeks he decides his first experience would be better with a sex worker. After all they have no expectations of a man apart from payment. John had found an escort site on the internet, which on first viewing seemed legit. Reading between the lines it was just a front for prostitutes. The arrangements had been made for Cassie to meet John at the Nocton Travel Lodge. His obsession with Andrea prevented him from even contemplating removing the shrine to shag a prostitute.

John pulled into the carpark of the hotel and waited for Cassie. He had sent a picture of himself to the agency along with his registration number so Cassie could spot him. John can see a women in her mid 20's wearing a black skirt, white top and a faded denim jacket walking towards him. As she walks her pony tail bounces up and down. She pauses at John's car door and looks at the image on her mobile phone before jumping into the passenger seat.

"Hi handsome! I would guess you are John."

John blushes and his ego is boosted by her comment. Cassie would give out any compliment she felt fit for £300 for two hours work.

"Nice to meet you."

Cassie pulls open her blouse a little.

"Do you like?"

"Lots."

Cassie gets out of the car and beckons john out. He gets out and Cassie grabs his hand. John goes up to the reception and asks for the key.

"Good evening."
You should have a room booked in the name of Bryant."

"Yes sir room 129. The key is here, your room is on the first floor. If you want breakfast, it's available until 10."

"Thank you."

The forty something year old receptionist had worked there long enough to know John wouldn't want breakfast. The signs were all there, no luggage, room booked in one name and the biggest of all Cassie had stayed the week before has a blonde not a brunette. John leads Cassie into the room he is very nervous. They both sit on the bed.

"Is there anything you would particularly like?"
"What do you mean?"

"Like your favourite position like doggie or me on top. Do you like lots of oral or even anal?"

"Could you speak to me in a soft Southern Irish accent?"

This was of course Andrea's accent.

"Whatever you want though I have got to say it is a little unusual. It's normally the classic English accent."

As Cassie starts to kiss John he soon becomes aroused. He fumbles away at Cassie's clothes until eventually she just takes them off herself. Cassie undresses john and pushes him down onto the pillow before mounting him. John gives a few thrusts but can already feel himself climaxing. He tries to stop himself but within moments he is done.

"Oh I am sorry."

"Don't worry. Do you think you are the only guy I have slept with who comes quickly?

John feels embarrassed, luckily this was just Cassie the escort and not his beloved Andrea.

"You have paid for two hours, so when you are ready we can go again. If you want I can just talk to you using the soft Southern Irish accent.

"Cassie I need to tell you something, I have never had sex before. I really don't know what to do."

"Well I tell you what, I will show you what women like and then you will feel confident enough to go out there and please the ladies."

John couldn't help but think Cassie was very kind and it was a shame she had to resort to sex to make a living.

The two hours passed and John was a much wiser man after Cassie's tutorage.

Over the next weeks John meets up with Cassie and fantasises about her being Andrea. The fake Southern Irish accent is augmented by Cassie wearing J'adore by Christian Dior. So now she sounds and smells like Andrea.

Andrea had now all but forgotten about the hand print and missing brush. It had been some months since her blood lust had been satisfied and she was ready to move on to the next victim.

Over at the MIT (Major investigation Team) headquarters, things had ground to a halt. The trawl of private CCTV, bus and dash cams had drawn a blank. The DCI in charge of all three missing person's cases was reviewing all the evidence prior to making her report to the ACC (Assistant Chief Constable) The results of that report would reflect in the budget and resources allocated to keep the investigations rolling.

It's late Saturday evening on a junction on the B112 road near Forchester. Andrea has parked her Mini up on the side of the road and driven a nail into a tyre to puncture it. She has jacked the car up and was struggling to get the wheel off. It is raining hard and she is waiting for a gallant passer-by to help her. After about 15 minutes she looks a sorry state her hair is soaked and her massacre is running down her face. Eventually a transit van pulls up behind her Mini. A young man in his mid to late 20s gets out of the van. He is wearing some kind of delivery driver uniform and a fluorescent vest. Andrea puts on her best hopeless, scared abandoned female face and begs the stranger for help.

"Are you ok love?"

"No, I think I have got a nail in my tyre."

"Let's have a look."

"I have been out here ages I am drenched."

"There is a nail in the tyre alright. How long have you had the car?"

"About 8 months I think, why?"

"Mini's don't have a spare tyre. They come with a tyre weld that's blocks the hole until you get to a garage. Let me help you."

The young man pulls out the nail with some pliers he has in the van. He then uses the tyre weld to stop any air coming out.

"There you are love all done. You will need to take it to a garage."

"You was amazing."

"I wouldn't go that far, just happy to have been able to assist."

Andrea bends forward and kisses the young man on the cheek.

"You need to get home quickly, the tyre weld won't last forever."

Andrea gets back in her Mini and jots down the mobile number from the side of the van. She smirks to herself, knowing her quest for a new victim is going well. The young man drives off and waves. Andrea drives home and changes the wheel for a spare she has in the shed. She is far from the hopeless young women she has just portrayed.

The following evening she is sat on her bed playing with the lock knife and staring at a piece of paper with a hastily jotted mobile number on. After a moment or two's deliberation she reaches over to the side of the bed for her burner phone and begins to type.

"Good evening. It was so kind of you to help me last night. I just hope your gallantry hasn't left you with Phenomena."

To her surprise the messaged is returned almost immediately.

"It was a pleasure and only what I would expect a stranger to do for my mum or sister."

"I hope you don't think I am being to forward. I would like to buy you a drink to say thank you. Oh please forgive me for asking if you have a partner."

"No I don't at the moment and it would be a pleasure. "

Chapter 13
The white knight

"I was hoping you would say that. Perhaps the nail was a piece of good luck. Rescued by a good looking single man who is just my type."

"Fate works in strange ways."

"Do you know the Half-moon inn at Bowton?"

"I certainly do, it's a lovely place and does some top food."

"If you are free Thursday night."

"I can make myself free for a beautiful girl like you."

"Gallant and charming."

"What time do you want to meet?"

"Shall we say 8pm?"

"I will look forward to it."

The Half-moon inn wasn't of course any random pub. Andrea had chosen it for its remoteness and lack of CCTV. She is sly, cunning and forensically aware.

Thursday evening came and Andrea was going through her rituals. Locking knife under the pillow, covers on the mattress, fuller's earth under the bed and silk ties in the draw next to the bed.

She showers and puts on her Victoria's Secrets killer thong and matching bra. Tonight's outfit will consist of a pretty flowered pink dress and kitten heeled boots. She looked beautiful and demure. It's only a short drive to the pub and she pulls into the carpark. Moments later a taxi arrives and the young man gets out. He is wearing a pair of Levi jeans and a tight muscle fit T shirt, his hair is slicked back with gel and he looks slim and athletic.

"Wow you look even more amazing when all your makeup is fixed to your face rather than running down it."

Andrea blushes and smiles.

"Do you know what, we don't even know each other's names?"

"Oh yer. My names James."

"I am Andrea."

"Pleased to meet you Andrea."

James gently shakes Andreas hand before kissing her on the cheek.

"Shall we go in before it rains again?"

"What do you want to drink Andrea?"

"No, no, my treat I said I was buying you a drink."

James points out a niche craft ale.

"I will have a pint of that please."

"I will have a glass of Prosecco please and a pint of whatever that is."

Andrea leads James to a quiet corner of the pub and they sit down.

"So do you make a habit of rescuing maidens in distress?"

"To be honest you are my first maiden in distress."

James sneezes a number of times.

"Oh dear that's what you get for being helpful, the flu."

"You're worth every sneeze Andrea."

James sneezes again.

Andrea leans forward and whispers into James ear.

"With a cold like that, I think you need to go straight to bed."

Andrea stands up and pulls James to his feet.

"You're coming with me young man."

"Yes miss whatever you say."

Andrea leads James to her car and they get in. Once they are in the car Andrea kisses James kisses James passionately and guides his hand to her vagina. He pulls her thong to one side and his fingers enter her. She gives out a little moan. James stops to undo the buttons on his jeans. Andrea knocks his hand away.

"Not here."

Andrea pulls away from the pub in the Mini. Fifteen minutes later they arrive at Andreas and rush through the door tearing at each other's clothes as they make their way to Andrea's room.

"Let's see what you have got in there." Andrea pulls away at the buttons on James Levis. She puts her hand in his jeans and pulls out his penis. She starts to masturbate him and he licks her nipples.

"This is exciting, but I like it to be very exciting."

Andrea reaches for the pieces of silk and ties James's right wrist to the bed. As she moves his left wrist the locking knife falls out from under the pillow. James glances to the side and feels unnerved. He tries to free his right wrist. Andrea pushes his left wrist away and James starts to panic. Andrea is now sat on top of him and he struggles to move. In a desperate attempt to free himself he bites Andrea's thigh and she winces in pain. She knows that if he frees his wrist he will easily overpower her and escape. Still in pain from the now bleeding bite on her thigh, she reaches over to the bed side table. In one single frenzied movement, she picks up a glass Yankee candle jar and smashes it into the side of James's head. He loses consciousness and blood trickles from his right temple. Every cloud has a silver lining, she thinks to herself as she slips a plastic bag over his head and ties it. There will be no gushing of blood to clean up. James will just slowly suffocate, a nice clean painless death. Overnight James goes the way of all Andrea's victims as his body is engulfed by the flames of the furnace and turns to ashes. There will be more planting to be done at Doreen's over the next week. James had gone the way of most gallant knights who help out helpless maidens.

Within days James too is reported has a missing person. This was now the fourth young man to disappear in mysterious circumstances. Over at the MIT the DCI is drafting in extra officers to ramp up the investigations in light of recent events. Surely it wouldn't be long before the killer made the fatal mistake which lead to them being apprehended. In truth Andrea had just made one such mistake. She had wheeled James's body over to the Blacksmiths shop in full view of her covert camera. The evidence would be recorded for 28 days before it is taped over.

John's confidence in all things sexual had grown, thanks to Cassie. He was however still painfully shy in the presence of women and approaching Andrea for a date was still a distant dream. With his wing man dead, he would now have to do some studies on developing confidence on the internet. Like most things in life learning and doing are two completely different things. It had been some weeks since John had managed to get his picture of Andrea and he longed to see her again if only a fleeting glimpse.

John had chosen a cloudy night to carry out his latest reconnaissance mission on Andrea's cottage. He knew that the lack of moonlight would help him in his quest to remain undetected. He dresses in the black hoody and jeans he had previously worn. Wanting to keep to his normal M.O he parks the BMW a street away and walks to Andrea's. It is 3am and eerily quiet apart from the distant sound of an owl hooting. He once again walks down the side of the cottage reaching his way down the wall. He is oblivious to the fact he is managing to keep out of the site of Andrea's camera. As he turns the corner he is now in full view of the second camera. He looks up over the orangery to see that Andrea's bedroom window is closed as are the curtains. He decides that discretion is the better part of valour and turns around to go. He takes a step and then catches the bottom of his jeans on a rosebush. As he pulls his leg away he trips over a ceramic plant pot which smashes to the floor. He scrabbles to his feet and his hood falls as he runs away. John's pulse is racing as he sprints in the direction of his car.

The next day Doreen received yet another unexpected delivery of plants from the garden centre. She obviously knew who they were from. By early evening Andrea had changed into her gardening scruffs and was making her way to Doreen's. Andrea knocks on Doreen's door and moments later she appears.

"Hello Doreen did you get your presents?"

"I did but why are you buying me even more plants?"

"When we spoke last week about your garden, you said you always wanted to have an orchard. Well I have been on line and apparently an orchard is three or more fruit trees. So I have bought you an apple tree, a pear tree and a cherry tree. Once I have planted them you will have an orchard."

"You are so thoughtful Andrea."

"Have you seen any cats or foxes around?"

"Why?"

"This morning that lovely ceramic pot you gave me was on the floor and broken."

"No but I did hear something at about 3am this morning. I was on my way to the toilet and thought I heard something break."

"I will take a look on my cameras."

"I don't think foxes specialise in stealing knickers from washing lines."

Over the next two hours Andrea creates and orchard for Doreen and extends her cemetery.

On Andreas return home she is anxious to look at her CCTV. She views the rear facing camera in real time from 0250am until 0310am. At 0301 a figure wearing all black comes into view. He is wearing a black hoody. He falls and as he does his hood comes down and he looks directly at the camera. Andrea talks to herself under her breath.

"Bingo got yer."

She prints the image off and racks her brain trying to identify the intruder.

John is at work the next day with Martin.

"Sorry I am a bit late mate, I had to drop my daughter off at her nursery."

"No worries pal. Which one does she go to?"

"Big World, on Denton Street."

"Oh yer, I know it, a kid once ran out from their playground in front of my car"

Martin was now thinking about the picture he had seen in John's wallet. He was pretty much convinced it was the nursery nurse at Big World. Amanda or something like that.

Over at Big World most of the children had gone on a day trip to the zoo, leaving Andrea and Mags to change displays and tidy chaotic stock rooms.

"You won't believe this Mags, I had an intruder last night."

"That sounds like another euphemism to me."

"No I woke up this morning to find a broken pot around the back of the cottage. Doreen told me she heard a breaking noise at about 3am. I checked my CCTV and saw someone around the back wearing dark clothing."

"Are you going to report it to the police?"

"Probably, but they had their hood up and you can't see their face."

"Do you think this could be the person who stole your knickers?"

"Possibly it's all a bit scary to be honest."

"Like I said if you feel scared you can stay over for a few nights."

"Thanks Mags but has I said I aren't into threesomes."

"No need to worry about that anymore."

"Why what's happened?"

Chapter 14
The female of the species is deadlier than the male

"It's over. Rob was at mine and had gone to the toilet. He had a text and I couldn't help but look. It was from his ex-Amy. They are quite clearly still involved sexually. He was just like most men, happy to get it when and where he can. I threw his clothes out of the window and told him to fuck off."

"Mags what can I say?"

"There's not a lot anybody can say. He was just a first class wanker."

"I bet your gutted babe he seemed so nice."

"Oh well, plenty more fish in the sea."

"I can feel another night out coming on, now my wing women is no longer loved up."

"It's great having no kids, but if I knock over one more pot of glue I will go mad."

They both laugh and the dower mood is lifted for now.

The day passes by quite quickly until all hell breaks loose when the children return at 3.30. The coach had been delayed and lots of parents were anxious about their loved ones. One of the last children to be picked up was Martins little girl.

"Hi there Mr Richards. Abby is just getting her things together she won't be long."

Martin is contemplating asking Andrea about the photo, when Abby appears.

"Come on chick lets go. I think there is a Happy Meal at McDonalds with your name on it."

"How do they know my name daddy?"

"They just do sweetie."

"See you tomorrow Abby."

"Amanda is it?"

"Nearly, Andrea,"

"Before I go I want to ask you a question. It might sound strange."

"I work with a guy called John Bryant. Do you know him?"

"I don't think so what does he look like."

"He's in his mid-thirties with short slightly wavy blonde hair and blue eyes."

"No it doesn't ring a bell. Why?"

"I shouldn't really say, but he had a photo in his wallet and it looked a lot like you."

"It must be some other stunningly hot blonde."

They both laugh but Andrea feels uneasy.

Later that day John is at home. He has photo shopped a picture of himself laid next to the naked Andrea. He is now fantasising and masturbating himself again, while sniffing the J'adore soaked bunch of Andrea's hair. He finishes himself off and smears the seamen over a picture of her face. Feeling sexually gratified he goes to shower. He appears a few minutes later and curls up on his bed naked clutching the J'adore soaked hair to his face. He feels at peace and soon falls asleep.

Andrea is now at home and making herself a coffee. Her mind thinks back to the conversation she had with Martin. Why would he think that a random picture his colleague had was her. She picks up the picture of the random intruder, she had printed off from her CCTV. The image is slightly fuzzy but it could be him. For any women having a strange stalker was a danger, for Andrea it could be a disaster. There was no way she could even contemplate going to the police. She would just have to deal with the situation herself. Maybe her next victim had selected himself. On the plus side he would get a brief taste of what he always wanted. Andrea knew she would have to tread carefully, because if she made things to obvious she would make herself a credible suspect.

The next day Martin feels a little uncomfortable in the presence of John because of what he had said to Andrea. Once again a technician comes in to take a breakfast order.

"Do either of you want a sandwich this morning?"

"Bacon, egg, Sausage and tomato for me please."

"What about you John?"

"Bacon with brown sauce please pal."

John takes his wallet from his jacket.

"Put it away it's my shout."

As John goes to his jacket to replace his wallet, the buzzer rings and he has to go through to deal with a customer at the counter. He leaves his wallet on the side. Once John and the technician are out of the room, curiosity gets the better of Martin. He opens the wallet and takes a look. Right at the back of the wallet slipped in behind a credit is the photo. He slips it out and takes a quick look. For some reason the photo doesn't look quite right. The girl in the photo was definitely Andrea though. He quickly replaces the photo as John walks back in.

Andrea had rung in sick and was having a day off from Big World. She had watched Martin drop his daughter off and followed him to Brookes. She now knew her mysterious stalker worked there. Andrea walks into the dealership and takes a look around. A salesman approaches her and she has a brief conversation about the Focus ST. As she is talking to the salesman she notices a display with pictures of all the staff and their names. Having made a promise to the salesman to call in at the weekend to have her car appraised for a part exchange she peruses the pictures. John Bryant (Parts Controller) this had confirmed her suspicions that John was indeed the stalker.

That evening she is sat on her laptop interrogating social media. She types in the name John Bryant. There are 27 recorded on Facebook and it takes her sometime to select each profile picture in turn to find him. It doesn't help that some people's profiles don't have pictures of them or completely unrealistic Avatars. Having located he prey on Facebook she pauses before sending him a friend request.

Over at John's he is watching a documentary on YouTube about the crusades. Though his interest in all things religious had died with his mother's suicide he had an interest in the holy warriors known has the Knights Templar. At first he doesn't even notice the Facebook notification on his mobile. The documentary finishes and he picks up his phone to check out some historical facts on the internet. At this point he notices the Facebook friend's request. As he reveals the identity of the request sender he is taken aback. He presses the accept button and is heart skips a beat. Perhaps there is a god after all and his dads obsession with all things religious had lead him to this moment. This could be the start of something beautiful or maybe not. Andrea sends a wave over to John and he waves back. Andrea replies with a message.

"Hello there I sent you a friend's request, because I thought you looked interesting."

John is contemplating what to put. He doesn't want to appear too keen, he is desperate to make a good impression.

"I am glad you sent me a request because you look amazing."

"I see from your about info that you live in the same town has me."

"Yes, Nocton the centre of the universe."

"What do you do for a living?"

"I work at a garage called Brookes has a parts controller. What about you?"

"Oh nothing very exciting I am a nursery nurse at Big World Nursery. The absolute heights of Nocton glamour."

"Ha, Ha, Kids they are sent to try us aren't they?

"Do you have any?"

"No I don't have any kids and I live on my own."

"No me neither. I have never met the right man to have a family with."

"He will be out there somewhere." John is contemplating sending a kiss on the end of the message. He decides against it, perhaps too much too soon.

"I just wish he would make himself known sooner rather than later."

John decides to play the long game and ends the conversation.

"You will have to excuse me, I need to get to bed because I am up early in the morning for work. Speak soon." On this occasion he finishes with a kiss.

"I will look forward to it XXX."

Three kisses and John is once again floating on air. John hadn't felt this happy since his relationship with Emily has a teenager. The next morning John woke up to another Facebook message from Andrea.

"Good morning it was lovely speaking yesterday and such a shame you had to go to bed. I hope you had a good night's sleep and woke up thinking of me xxx."

"I had a lovely sleep and I did think of you last night."

Of course, it would have been grossly inappropriate to say yes. I woke up at 2am and masturbated over a naked picture I took of you, through your bedroom window.

Andrea had a way of making herself desired which went way beyond her looks and amazing personality. It was pretty much true to say, she could have any man she wanted if she put her mind to it. John was like the fish gobbling up the ground bait just waiting to be hooked, gutted and fried.

"I hope you have a wonderful day and I can't wait to message you later x."

"I will wish the day away so I can hear from you x"

John's drive to work took him past Big World. As he drove past he caught a glimpse of Andrea in the playground but to his disappointment she didn't look round at him. He arrives at work early and is sat in his car. John takes out his picture of Andrea with his superimposed image on. He is staring at it, hoping and praying that one day it would be replaced with a real image of them as a couple. Martin has also arrived at work early and is stood near to John's driver's door watching him staring at the picture. He knocks on the driver's window and John looks round before hastily shoving the picture back into his wallet.

"Are you coming in mate, or are you just going to spend all day locked in the car has some kind of protest?"

John opens the window to talk to Martin.

"Sorry mate my mind was elsewhere and yes I am going to stay here."

"It was my turn to make the brews too."

"In that case I am coming?"

"What kind of a crap protest was that?"

"A bloody thirsty one."

John gets out and walks into work with Martin.

Throughout the day Andrea had sent over the occasional kiss to John and in response John had gone back out to his car a number of times to stare at her photo. Every kiss installed more and more desire into John's mind.

Over at the MIT, there had been another break through. The Sat nav had been recovered from the burnt out Range Rover sport. After submission to a private company by the Digital Forensic Unit, they had managed to get the last programmed entry from it. The last location Harvey Miles had entered was on Dove Road, Nocton. Andrea couldn't have known that the sat nav survived the petrol tank blowing up and the subsequent inferno. Enquiries would now have to be carried out on Dove Road. All a little too close to home for Andrea.

That evening Andrea is laid in the bath, when the doorbell rings. She quickly hops out and puts on a dressing gown. Her hair is dripping everywhere as she goes downstairs. Andrea opens the door. Stood in front of her are two men, both suited and booted. One in his mid to late 30's the other in his early 50's, with a shaven head and greying well-trimmed beard. Round their necks are blue lanyards with the word police emblazoned on them. Hanging from them are the officers Warrant cards. The older officer's picture was obviously taken some years ago.

"Good evening, sorry to disturb you love. I am DS Crompton and this is DC Bennet from Nocton CID."

"Good evening officers, how can I help?"

"We are doing some enquiries into a missing person. A gentlemen named Harvey Mile visited this road on or around the 20th of July in the evening. He was driving a grey Range Rover Sport. The registration number was ND09 LTQ."

The more junior detective hands over two pictures to Andrea. One is a picture of Harvey taken from his passport photo. The other is an image of a grey Range Rover from the internet.

"Sorry I don't recall seeing either Mr Miles or the car. It's pretty quiet around here and we tend to keep ourselves to ourselves."

"You don't by chance have any CCTV cameras do you?"

"I have, but they were installed only a couple of weeks ago and they only cover the back and side of the cottage."

"In that case we will leave you to get on with your evening."

"Good night, I hope you have some success with your enquiries."

Andrea returned to her bath. She had no concerns about the police investigations, because there was nothing to lead the police to her doorstep other than routine enquiries. She still had her mind firmly set on putting an end to her stalker.

Next door the detectives are struggling to get a response from knocking on Doreen's door. Eventually the DS goes around the back to knock on the kitchen door. Doreen is making a cup of tea, when she sees the officer through the window. She has noticed the lanyard and warrant card. She opens the door.

"Good evening officer, how can I help you?"

"There's no pulling the wool over your eyes, I haven't even introduced myself yet.""

The detective affirms his identity by showing Doreen his warrant card.

"I am DS Crompton from Nocton CID. We are conducting some enquiries into a missing person."

"What makes you think I can help?"

"We have reason to believe the man in question visited this street in mid to late July."

The officer repeats the process of showing the pictures of the car and Harvey.

"Sorry love I can't say I have seen either. I don't really get out much and if I need anything Andrea next door helps me."

"Never mind. By the way your garden looks beautiful."

"Yes, Andrea next door does some planting for me. She says she uses a special compost."

"You are lucky to have her. Those roses and hydrangeas could win prizes they are amazing."

"Il will let her know you have admired her efforts. She puts a lot of soul into her gardening."

The office walks off and meets up with his colleague.

Andrea is laid in a fresh path with a glass of prosecco, tapping away at her burner phone.

"Good evening John I have been looking forward to speaking to you all day xxx."

"I am so happy to hear from you. You brighten my day and blow away the clouds."

John had pressed the send button before he had the chance to realise how corny that line sounded.

"What are you doing? I am laid in the path drinking prosecco and thinking of you."

"I am just watching TV and eating biscuits."

Andrea takes a picture of herself in the bath using the timer function on her I-phone. After a number of attempts she eventually gets it right. She is laid back using the bubbles in the bath like some kind of plunge bra, to show off her cleavage. Andrea's right knee is bent to show off her slender leg. She smiles to herself and presses the send button. John opens up the picture and his heart fills with happiness. Surely Andrea must be interested in him, to send such a provocative picture.

"Want can I say about your picture apart from those taps are lovely."

John really didn't know what to reply, so he tried to add a little humour to the presiding's

Andrea knows she has the upper hand and is confident she can reel him in at will.

"I need to go now because I need to moisturise my body. Some parts are hard to reach and I could really do with some help! XXX."

John replies with a simple kiss.

Feeling turned on, he begins to masturbate over the picture of Andrea in the bath.

Andrea throws her phone on the bed and considers her next move. It was pretty much like taking candy from a baby.

The next morning Andrea sends a picture of herself naked in bed with her breasts exposed just above the nipple line by a bed sheet. She is totally unaware that John had a more explicit picture of her.

John is running late for work and frustratingly has the time to send "A good morning X."

An hour later Andrea arrives at Big World and is talking to Maggie.

"Good morning Mags."

"Good morning love. I have been looking forward to seeing you."

"You see me nearly every day."

"I have got some news."

"I bet it's something to do with a guy."

"You are wise my friend for someone so young."

"I aren't wise Mags, you are smiling from ear to ear."

"I am really happy."

"So give me the sordid details."

"I met this guy last weekend at Halfords of all places. My car had a bulb out and he fitted it for me."

"What he works for Halfords."

"No he was just in there and saw me looking at bulbs."

"A white knight hey."

"Something like that. I took him to Costa for a coffee to say thanks."

"Have you seen him since?"

"Not yet, we have face timed each other every night though. He just seems really nice."

"So will the lucky pants be getting an outing?"

"I don't want to appear to eager babe."

"I hope he's not another Rob."

"You mean Rob the knob."

"That's him. I don't want men messing around with my bestie."

"I don't think they dare, you might kill them."

"No not me, I don't think I could ever kill anyone."

"What about you Andrea, anybody on the scene."

"I have had a few Facebook messages from a guy. Looks wise, he's not really my cup of tea."

"Oh well, maybe just a good friend."

"Men and women can have friends of the opposite sex without any shenanigans."

"Yes, and the moons made of cream cheese."

"Fair point, any man would want to shag you, you're stunning."

"Just because I kissed you once on a drunken night out."

"I aren't gay or bi Andrea, but if I was you would be getting it."

John is also on top of the world at work. It seemed like all his hopes and aspirations for him and Andrea was coming true. He had spent 9 hours day dreaming and Martin was losing patience with his lack of effort. Every time a customer came in, he was gazing into space while martin served them.

"Right that's it, let's get locked up."

"It's not been a bad day really."

"Not for you mate. I have worked my arse off while you have bumbled around."

"Sorry mate, I have got something on at home and it's been on my mind."

"Ok mate, but please, please be on it tomorrow."

"I will, good night mate."

John is in the car literally seconds, before he is looking at Andrea's pictures on his phone. Besotted doesn't begin to describe his feelings towards her.

Chapter 15
Falling down the trap door

John is sat in his car for just over an hour, eventually his concentration is halted by a message alert. The object of his affections has just had just sent him a message.

"I am in town at the moment and would like to meet you. What do you think? XXX"

John's fingers cannot type quickly enough.

"Where and what time?"

"In 20 minutes time, in the Costa coffee on the High Street."

"I will see you soon. XXX."

Sod's law dictates that the traffic on the way to town is bumper to bumper and John is feeling frustrated. There is a loud beep and the squealing of brakes as John pulls out into the traffic without making proper observations. Luckily no one is hurt and John can carry on with his journey. He can feel the tingle of excitement and anticipation as he pulls into the car park near to Costa. John walks the few hundred yards to Costa at pace, accidentally bumping into a number of people on the busy high street. Eventually he makes it to the door of the coffee shop and takes a deep breath before going in. Andrea is nowhere to be seen. John buys a Vanilla Latte and a slice of lemon drizzle cake and takes one of the seats usually occupied by Andrea and Mags. His heart is skipping and he feels anxious. John decides to look at his phone to kill some time and calm his nerves. After a few minutes he is interrupted by the most gentle of soft Southern Irish accents.

"Room for a little one John?"

John looks up from his phone and melts at the sight of Andreas beautiful eyes.

"Hi. Please sit down"

"Sorry I am late, the traffic was awful."

"No. worries. I haven't been here long myself."

Andrea sits down next to John and shuffles along so they are quite close.

"It's lovely to meet you in the flesh rather than just a picture on social media."

"You look even more amazing in real life."

Andrea blushes and smiles.

"It's strange to think we have all these friends on social media, but most we will never ever meet."

"I have seen you in here before Andrea. You were sat in these exact same seats a few weeks ago with a friend."

"What was she like?"

"Brunette, probably in her early 40s."

"Oh yer, that's my best friend Maggie. We work together at Big World nursery."

"I think you had been shopping or something."

"It would have been us. I was shopping for knickers."

Andrea thinks back to her shopping trip with Mags to buy knickers and how it was highly probable that the man in front of her had cost her £28 for the new pair.

"So tell me a little more about yourself Andrea."

"There's not a lot to say to be honest. I have been single for about 8 years now and I live in a lovely detached cottage on Dove Road."

"How come someone who looks like you is single?"

"I just generally seem to attract all the wrong kind of men. They either want a quick fling and no commitment or they love themselves much more than they could ever love me."

"That's sad you deserve someone nice."

"That's why when I read your profile on Facebook, I contacted you."

"That's pretty flattering Andrea."

"I just hope looks can't be too deceiving."

"Cheeky. No I am a kind genuine guy with lots of love to give."

"We will have to see what happens. I am open to a relationship and commitment with the right person. Not to mention the fact that the chemical clock is ticking. Nobody will want to marry the old baron spinster of Nocton."

"You are far from that, I am sure."

"Well I need a man to protect me. You won't believe what happened a few weeks ago."

Andrea is deliberately trying to mention the stolen knickers incident, to force some kind of reaction from John.

"Why what happened?"

"Someone stole a pair of knickers from my washing line. I was buying replacements when you saw me."

John looks like a child who has been told off for eating all the chocolate and denied it even though they had chocolate around their face.

"That's disgusting. Maybe it was just kids."

"No, I recon some dirty perverts got them hanging from their bed post right now."

John takes a gulp and tries to change the subject.

"Do you want anything else to eat or drink?"

"I will have to decline that kind offer because I really need to go now. I have got a hot date with my next-door neighbour at 6."

Johns face looks disappointed.

"The hot dates with my 80-year-old neighbour Doreen. She's invited me around for tea."

The couple stand up and make their way to the door.

"I will message you later, it's been lovely meeting you."

Andrea kisses John on the cheek.

"See you soon."

For the first time ever, Andrea was in turmoil over a potential victim. She genuinely liked John and the thought of killing him was playing with her conscience. She could not however risk his stalking leading the police to her door to discover her ghastly crimes. On her return home she pulls an old box of photos from the back of a cupboard. At the front of the box was an old manila envelope. This contained a single picture of a forty something man in the 1980s, holding the hand of a little blonde haired girl with pigtails and a blue gingham dress. The little girl was Andrea and the man her uncle Ian. As a little girl she had seen her uncle try and rape her mum. Neither Andrea nor her mum ever mentioned it to her dad. This was the motivation behind lowering men to their deaths with sex. Staring at the picture re-kindled the events in her mind and increased her resolve.

John decided not to message Andrea while she was having tea with Doreen. In truth the whole Doreen thing had been a fabrication to leave John frustrated at not getting more time with Andrea.

 The next morning Andrea goes into work to find one of the classroom windows had been broken into and some damage done inside the nursery. There is glass on the window ledge and some on the floor. She reaches down to pick up a piece of glass and cuts her hand. The blood dripping from Andreas hand is adding to blood which is already on the floor. Mags grabs some paper towels and rushes over to Andrea.

"Give me your hand that looks bad."

Mags presses the paper towels onto her hand.

"Ouch that hurts."

"I don't want you bleeding to death."

"Let's have a look."

Andreas has a 2 inch gash near her thumb.

Chapter 16
Just a matter of time

"I think you might need a couple of stiches."

Another member of staff takes Andrea to A and E.

Meanwhile the nursey manager has called the police and a patrol officer attends.

"Good morning I understand you have had a break in."

"Yes, I think they got in through class 3's window. I will take you to the class. There are no children in it today."

The nursery manager and the police officer make their way to the classroom.

"This is Maggie. I will leave you in her capable hands."

"Pleased to meet you Maggie, I am PC Richards from the Nocton neighbourhood policing team. I understand you have had some kind of break in."

"Yes, we came in this morning to find that window broken and some blood on the floor."

"Is there any other damage?"

"Yes the sinks had paper towels stuffed into the plugholes and the taps left on. There is some water damage to the corridor carpets."

"There is quite a lot of blood here. I will have to get Scenes of Crimes out to exam it and dust down the windows."

"That's fine. Just one think before you do."

"What's that?"

"My colleague Andrea cut her hand picking up some glass and her blood is also on the floor."

"It's not a problem SOCO can do an elimination DNA test. What's Andrea's full name?"

"Oh it's Andrea Walker."

The officer scrolls down some details before putting his radio to his mouth."

"Control from 1342."

"Go ahead 1342."

"Can I have SOCO to Big World nursery please? Can you add the following details to the log? I will be criming this has a commercial burglary, with the crime number to follow. An elimination DNA sample needs taking from a member of staff called Andrea Walker. Her blood is at the scene along with that of the possible offenders.

"All received 1342."

Two hours later Andrea returns with her hand glued and a small dressing over the wound.

The Scenes of crimes officer has dusted for prints and taken swabs from the classroom floor.

"Are you by any chance Andrea Walker?"

"Yes I am."

"Because your blood is on the floor along with that of the offenders I need to take an elimination DNA test from you."

Andrea is inwardly reluctant to take the test, because she doesn't want the police having her DNA. However she knows it would seem odd to refuse. To the best of her knowledge she hadn't left incriminating DNA anywhere.

"That's fine it's not like I am some kind of master criminal."

A few minutes later the DNA test is complete. Just a buccal swab on the inside of each cheek.

"That was pretty painless, if anything it ticked."

"Can you just sign to confirm I took the DNA from you?"

The SOCO officer leaves leaving Andrea and Mags in the empty classroom.

"Wow that was an exciting morning."

"It might have been for you. All I got from it was, nearly two hours in A and E and a mouth scrape."

"I wonder who the little bastards are."

"It's one thing breaking in to steal something and another just breaking in to commit damage."

"There is just no respect these days"

For the rest of the day Andrea feels like the spectre of the DNA sample is hanging over her. It will not deter her from carrying out her next murder though. On her return home she messages John.

"I hope you have had a great day at work, sadly I haven't because I hurt my hand. XXX"

"You are kidding me. I hope you are ok."

"I cut my hand on some glass and had to go to A and E."

"If I was there I would kiss it better."

"Kiss what better? XXX"

"Your hand silly."

When it comes to flirting, Andrea is a grand master. Her every word is carefully crafted to bring about John's demise. She is sat on her bed opening and closing the lock knife and occasionally running the blade over her uncle Ian's photo.

You can kiss me when you see me next."

"Where?"

"Anywhere you like."

John is instantly turned on and is fantasising about Andrea, whilst she is messaging him.

"Anywhere?"

"Yes anywhere."

John begins to masturbate. He knows it is wrong but he cannot help himself. Andrea can take him to a sexual high just with words.

"So when can I see you again Andrea?"

"Saturday evening if you fancy it. Perhaps we can get some time alone and entertain each other."

"I can't wait."

"Me neither. I can't tell you what I am doing now, but on Saturday I can show you."

John sighs as he ejaculates.

"I will send you a little clue."

Andrea sends over a picture of two fingers. From this John forms the opinion that she too is masturbating. In truth she is still sat on the bed running the blade of the knife over Ian's photo.

"I think I know what you are doing, but I would like you to tell me."

"Sorry I need to go now but on Saturday you can help me, if you're a lucky boy."

"Ok goodnight."

Andrea does not reply. It's all part of her end game for John. If only he hadn't become so obsessed with the wrong person. His fate was sealed from the moment Andrea saw his image on the CCTV. It would soon be time for Doreen's garden to acquire some more plants.

Over the next few days the only messages John receives are of the same two fingers, every couple of hours. He messages her, but she does not reply.

Over at the Major Investigation Team a young detective picks up a call from the National DNA database offices.

"Good morning, Can I speak to someone from the team dealing with the disappearance of Matthew Giles."

"Yes its DC Young speaking, I am dealing with Operation Abingdon, which is the disappearance of Matthew amongst others."

"We have a match for a previously unknown DNA hit found in Matthews's car."

"That's fantastic news. Can you give me the details?"

"The DNA was matched with an elimination sample taken from the scene of a burglary. The female is an Andrea Walker of Dove Road, Nocton."

"Can you email that information over please?"

"Certainly."

"Cheers thank you,"

The detective walks over to the SIO's door and knocks.

"Come in."

"Ma'am, good news."

"What's that?"

"I have just had a call about a DNA match on a swab taken from Matthew Giles car."

"Tell me more."

"The DNA matches an elimination test taken from the scene of a burglary. It comes down to a female called Andrea Walker, she lives on Dove Road. It's the last destination on Harvey Miles's sat nav."

"Can you speak to DS Garner about organising a briefing in the morning? I think we might just have enough to get a magistrate to sign a warrant.

Saturday morning comes around and John still hadn't had any contact with Andrea, apart from the finger pics. He is beginning to wonder if she was just playing him and how cruel it would be if that were the case. It's a very thin line between love and hate and the last thing John wanted was to hate Andrea. The hours pass and it is now mid-afternoon. There has been nothing from Andrea not even the finger pics. John is engrossed in the football scores when his phone beeps.

"Sorry I haven't been in touch, I am a very naughty girl and wanted to leave you wondering if our date would ever go ahead."

"I just hoped you wouldn't break my heart."

"I am going to play a game with you."

"I like games."

"I want you to come to my cottage and you need to walk there because Doreen will quiz me if she sees your car."

"What time? Where do you live?"

"I live where shoes used to be made, but not shoes for you or me. On the road where the bird of peace should be. You need to be there no earlier than 6 and no later than 7. See you soon lover XXX"

"At least I have all afternoon to work it out. XXX"

John will obviously be there by 6pm. The silly puzzle was pointless for a man who had stolen souvenirs from her bedroom. He smiles to himself confident in the fact he will soon be with Andrea.

Andrea is at home and doing her pre-murder checks. Locking knife in place, Fullers earth and water proof Sheets. Once again a tinge of pity for John begins to pass over her. Not once had she felt even the smallest amount of compassion for her victims. She knew that even the slightest spark of compassion in John's company might lead to her making a un- rectifiable mistake.

At a little after 6pm the doorbell rings and Andrea goes to the door. She is wearing a short silk dressing gown and nothing else but a smile.

"Somebody is a very clever boy."

Of course Andrea expected his prompt arrival. Andrea quickly pulls John through the door and sits him down on the sofa.

"Would you like a drink, a glass of wine a beer maybe?"

"A beer would be wonderful."

Andrea trots off into the kitchen and returns with John's beer. He takes a quick swig.

"Don't drink your beer like that silly."

John gives Andrea a puzzled look.

Andrea opens her dressing gown and lets it slide off her shoulders, before sitting astride him. She then takes the beer from him and pours some down her neck and breasts.

"More like this."

Andrea directs Johns head to her neck and his hands to her breasts. He gently runs his fingers over her nipples and she begins to moan.

"That's taken care of my clothes, but what about yours."

Andrea pulls at John's belt and undoes it. She then leads him upstairs into the bedroom like a naughty dog.

"I think I need some of your beer."

Andrea undresses John and lays him out on the bed. She then gently pours a little beer into his mouth before pouring some onto his neck, chest and penis. Andrea reaches over to the bedside cabinet for a piece of silk which she ties over his eyes.

"I don't like people watching me drink."

John feels a little uncomfortable, though he relishes the thought of Andreas tongue passing over his body with only his sense of touch.

As Andrea's head gets close to his neck he can smell J'adore. He can feel her gently kissing his neck and licking the beer from him. The kisses move down to his chest and Andrea reaches under the pillow for the locking knife. She gently releases the blade and moves down to the head of his penis. HE can feel her breath on his skin has she begins to lick. The knife is in her hand and she is contemplating the best time to strike.

There is a deafening bang as the front door of the cottage falls from its hinges. Followed by a rumble of steps running up the stairs. John jumps up off the bed and pulls the silk from his eyes. Moments later he is joined at the side of the bed by three detectives in police body armour. Andrea is sat up in bed with the open locking knife in her hand. Two of the officers draw their batons.

"Police! Put the knife on the floor."

Andrea complies and a female detective offers her a coat to hide her modesty.

"Andrea Walker, I am arresting you on suspicion of murder." She is then cautioned.

She begins to sob uncontrollably and offers no reply.

Officers lead her to a waiting police vehicle.

John is allowed to dress and is taken to the MIT to give a statement. He is visibly shaking both from fear and the realisation that the object of his affections was a serial killer.

For a few fleeting moments he had everything he ever wanted.

"John, I know you have been through a lot today and we will be arranging for you to see a Force Medical officer before we take you home. The Senior Investigative Officer would like to meet you, because she thinks she might have known you some time ago."

Moments later a detective in her early 30s with a familiar smile enters the room.

"John this is Detective Chief Inspector Emily Watts, the SIO."

The story of a boy growing up in the 80s in a Christian family with a clergyman father. He is sent to a Church school and isolated from his friends. The untimely death of his mother destroys any bond he might still have with his father.

As an adult he is shy and lacks any confidence with the opposite sex. An unhealthy obsession with a nursery nurse will lead to his life being put in danger. An intervention by a past love will save the day at the eleventh hour.

Contents

Chapter 1
In the shadows of God

Chapter 2
Goodbye Mum

Chapter 3
My Broken heart

Chapter 4
Just an ordinary girl

Chapter 5
Smoke and mirrors

Chapter 6
Daniels driving

Chapter 7
A lamb to the slaughter

Chapter 8
Obsession

Chapter 9
Dashing from the date

Chapter 10
Maggie pulls

Chapter 11
An uneasy feeling

Chapter 12
Experience is everything

Chapter 13
The white knight

Chapter 14
The female of the species is deadlier than the male

Chapter 15
Falling down the trap door

Chapter 16
Just a matter of time

Printed in Great Britain
by Amazon